PINKERTON GUNMAN

Nolan, a drifter, having left his job in
honse's Travelling Circus, applies for a
st in the Pinkerton Detective Agency. His
nge of occupation also means a change
the worse in his life. He is involved in a
on fight and finds himself sentenced to
years' hard labour. Ben manages to
pe from the chain gang, but becomes
lved with a gang of outlaws. Then he
mixed up in a robbery which is
plicated by the presence of a preacher's
tiful daughter. The final shoot-out ends
Ben's life hanging by a thread.

PINKERTON GUNMAN

PINKERTON GUNMAN

by

Ted Rushgrove

Dales Large Print Books
Long Preston, North Yorkshire,
BD23 4ND, England.

British Library Cataloguing in Publication Data.

Rushgrove, Ted
    Pinkerton gunman.

    A catalogue record of this book is
    available from the British Library

    ISBN   1-84262-352-4 pbk

First published in Great Britain 2004 by Robert Hale Limited

Copyright © Ted Rushgrove 2004

Cover illustration © Longaron by arrangement with
Norma Editorial S.A.

Published in Large Print 2005 by arrangement with
Robert Hale Ltd.

Dales Large Print is an imprint of Library Magna Books Ltd.

Printed and bound in Great Britain by
T.J. (International) Ltd., Cornwall, PL28 8RW

CHAPTER 1

The man rode slowly up to the farmhouse. He was riding an old grey stallion and he had the unmistakable air of a person who has spent a considerable time in the saddle. His clothes were well-worn and the only thing about him that appeared to be in pristine condition were the two guns in their holsters. Their handles gleamed in the late afternoon sunshine.

Mr Nolan watched him with growing apprehension. It was unusual for strangers to come this far off the beaten track. His farm was about half a mile from the nearest neighbour and they were both far away from the road between Crossville and Fort Munro.

The man was now about a couple of hundred yards away. Nolan knew that this was the time to make his move. If he hesitated any longer the man would be near the barns. If he was a stranger intent on causing trouble then he would be able to dive behind the buildings. Once there he would be able to get access to the back of the farmhouse.

Nolan stepped outside the front door. He held a Winchester at the ready.

'That's far enough, mister,' he shouted.

The stranger reined in his horse. The man facing him might have grey hair but he had the determined appearance of a person who would defend his property, come what may.

'I take it you don't want to hear my proposition,' he said with a smile.

Nolan was rather taken aback by the remark. He had expected the stranger to ask for some chow or maybe some water for the horse. But a proposition was an entirely novel approach.

'Stay where you are. You can say your piece from there.' The rifle moved slightly to add a threat to the command.

'My name is Glen Hillier. I'm a representative of the Wells Railroad Company. I'm selling their stock. If you want to make a fortune in a short while I'd advise you to buy some. I've just sold some to your neighbour, Stan Wilkins.'

Nolan hesitated. He knew that people were making small fortunes by buying railway stock. It was common gossip when he took the pony and trap into Crossville to sell his chickens and afterwards called in one of the saloons. The talk was that there was a proposed line between Crossville and Fort Munro. This would certainly open up this part of the county, which at the moment was largely neglected by the big companies.

'How much stock did Stan buy?'

'Five hundred dollars' worth.'

If Stan had bought any stock then the Hillier must be a genuine salesman. Stan would never buy anything without going into the ins and outs of the transaction. He was known as the meanest skinflint around.

'Have you got the document he signed?'

'Sure. Here it is.' Hillier fished in his saddlebag and produced a document.

Nolan realized that it could be any document. He was too far away to read it. He lowered his rifle slightly. The gesture was not lost on Hillier.

'What did Stan have to say about the stock?'

'At first he wouldn't consider the idea. Then when I pointed out that he would be guaranteed to double his money in a year he became interested. When I told him that if he let that money accumulate, in three years' time he could be worth as much as five thousand dollars, he became very interested indeed.'

Nolan squinted into the late afternoon sun. He mentally weighed the proposition. A profit of $5000 in three years time sounded great. He wasn't getting any younger. Of course if Ben had stayed things would have been different. They might even have bought more land and extended the farm. But Ben had buggered off two years ago after they had had one row too many. Now he was left to run the farm with a couple of hired hands. But they had gone into Crossville to attend a funeral, which was why he was on his own facing the stranger.

'Look, we can't talk like this, Mr Nolan,' stated Hillier, reasonably. 'Can we go inside the house? I'll show you the documents. Then you can make your own mind up.'

'Stan told you my name was Nolan?'

'That's right.' Hillier shifted in the saddle.

Nolan wavered. The only thing that prevented him from inviting Hillier into the house was the condition of his revolvers. They looked the kind of weapons which had been lovingly cared for. On the other hand he could be mistaken and the guns could be in pristine condition only because they were new.

'I can't stay here all day,' said Hillier, irritably. 'Either you let me into the house so that you can look at the documents or I'll turn back now.'

Nolan came to a decision. 'You can come in,' he said. 'But no tricks. I'll be keeping you covered.'

In the house Hillier spread the documents over the kitchen table.

'This is the share transfer document that Wilkins signed,' he said.

It was while Nolan was leaning forward, trying to decipher the name on the transfer deed that there was a flurry of movement. Before Nolan could turn Hillier had produced one of his gleaming revolvers. Nolan's last thought before the bullet hit him was that he had been right after all.

CHAPTER 2

The two men sat staring at the door which had just closed behind their visitor. Neither spoke for a short while. Eventually Burke said:

'I don't think he's suitable.' Burke, who was seated behind the desk, was a heavy-featured middle-aged man with a large black moustache. It was an intimidating moustache which sometimes made his subordinates quail, particularly when it seemed to bristle with anger. Now, however, his subordinate, Grey, was not in awe of it. He was seated at the side of Burke's desk and his face wore a thoughtful expression.

'He's good with a gun,' Grey stated. Like his boss he too was middle-aged. He had an undistinguished face which was useful at times when he was required to tail a suspect. It was the sort of face which would easily melt into a crowd if the person he was tailing happened to turn round suddenly.

'I'll give him that,' Burke concurred. Nolan had drawn his gun at his request to show how quick he was.

'We're short of good field men who can handle a gun.' Grey pursued the idea.

'There's something about him I don't trust,' said Burke, lighting a thin cigar. 'Do you think he told us the truth about his background?'

'Like working in a circus for the past two years and travelling around from place to place? Well it certainly means we won't be able to check on him. If he had lived in one town we would have been able to contact the town's sheriff and see whether he knew anything about him.'

'Or like him being in jail recently,' suggested Burke.

'Yes, that thought had crossed my mind too,' said Grey, thoughtfully. 'I don't suppose we'd be able to contact the circus-owner he said he was last working for?'

'Alphonse's Travelling Troupe. No, they could be anywhere. If they really exist at all.'

'So if we do hire him we'll have to take him at his word,' suggested Grey.

Burke tapped some of the ash from his cigar into an ash-tray. The office was sparsely furnished with only the desk and the three chairs being the items of furniture. There was no carpet on the polished wooden floor. The originator of the Chicago enterprise, Allan Pinkerton, had been a thrifty Scotsman. And although he had joined the heavenly hosts some years before, the air of austerity still prevailed in the offices.

'If we weren't so short of field men I wouldn't consider him,' said Burke. 'But needs must when the devil drives. We'll get him back in.'

Grey went to the door. 'Come back in, Mr Nolan.'

A tall slim figure followed Grey into the office. He was in his late twenties and had the sort of face which many women would consider handsome. He had steely grey eyes set in a finely chiselled face. He had a firm jaw and a positive air about him but without the swagger of someone who was over-confident.

'Sit down, Mr Nolan.' Burke indicated the spare chair.

Nolan sat. He stared at Burke expectantly.

'There are just one or two points about your application I'd like to go over with you. You say your last job was with a travelling circus?'

'That's right.'

'What exactly did you do in the circus?'

'I threw knives.'

Both men registered surprise. 'Who was the target?' demanded Grey.

'The boss's wife, a French lady named Marie.'

'Are you a good knife-thrower?' asked Burke.

'I think so. I never nicked her while I was throwing knives at her.'

'You liked working in the circus?' ventured Grey.

'I was happy there for a while. Then in the end I began to get restless. I decided it was time to move on.'

'Would that have something to do with a woman?' demanded Burke. He was not a detective for nothing. A man with the handsome features of Nolan would surely have at least one woman who had fallen in love with him.

Nolan smiled. It was the first time his expression had altered since he came into the office.

'There was an – incident – with a lady, yes.'

'What was the name of the lady?' pursued Burke.

For a moment it looked as though Nolan was going to refuse to answer. Then he shrugged.

'It was Marie. She was the boss's wife.'

Burke's face broke into a smile. Grey, who was a regular churchgoer and who was against extra-marital relationships, frowned.

'So that was why you had to leave,' stated Burke.

'It was either that or getting shot by Alphonse. He had a quick temper.'

Grey, who was annoyed at the apparent way Burke had accepted the truth of Nolan's statements, said:

'What were the names of the others who worked in the circus?'

Nolan didn't hesitate. 'There was Lord Anders, he was an Englishman who had a conjuring act. He also cheated at cards. I lost quite a few dollars to him.' He smiled ruefully at the memory. 'Then there was Kitty, she was nicknamed the Irish Thrush – she had a nice voice. There was Madame Lavinsky, the fortune teller and there were the two dwarfs, Tom and Treena. That was the lot. It was only a small circus.'

'So you were forced to leave because of your relationship with the owner's wife?' demanded Grey, worrying the cause like a kitten with a ball of wool.

'That's right,' said Nolan, dismissively. He had already worked out that it was what Burke said, not Grey, which was going to count in the end.

Burke stubbed out his cigar. It was obvious that the time for a decision had arrived. He coughed to emphasize the importance of the moment. Grey glanced at his boss. He guessed that the decision was going to be in favour of hiring the two-timer.

He was right. Burke announced:

'You're hired, Nolan. But if you step out of line you will be instantly dismissed. Not only that but we have a lot of influence with the sheriffs around the country. You would find it difficult to find another job. Do I make myself clear?'

'Yes,' replied Nolan. 'You can rely on me to be a faithful Pinkerton agent.'

Can we? wondered Grey, as he went with him into the outer office to arrange for his badge of office and to settle his details of payment.

CHAPTER 3

Fort Munro was a thriving, bustling town. It was a town which was growing rapidly, thanks to the railroad which had arrived there three years before. It had five churches but these were easily outnumbered by the saloons which, at the last count, had reached twenty-four. It also had several banks, livery stables, coffee houses, a variety of shops, two schools and one jail. The one building it did not possess was an opera house. But one man hoped soon to remedy that. His name was Alphonse.

When the circus had been forced to break up due to his discovery of his wife's adultery with the treacherous, snake in the grass, Nolan, Alphonse was forced to consider his future. It was obvious that it did not rest with the circus, since Nolan's knife-throwing act with Marie as the target was the climax of the evening's entertainment. If that was taken away then the whole programme collapsed. Added to which Lord Anders quickly followed Nolan's example in leaving the circus – taking with him one of Alphonse's prized stallions.

So Alphonse had to reconsider his future. It only took him a short while to come up with the idea of building an opera house. It was a venture which was close to his heart since he was half-Italian, and everybody knew that Italians loved singing. Building an opera house would take time, need careful planning and above all, need a loan from the bank to finance it.

First of all he had to dismiss his companions in the circus. It was not an easy task. They had been together for the past four years and they had come to regard him as a father figure. If any of them had troubles they would come to him to ask his advice. He couldn't always come up with the right answers but the fact that they would come to him meant a lot to him.

There were some tearful scenes the evening when he told them that it was the last show. The dwarfs, Treena and Tom were obviously heartbroken at receiving their last payment. Kitty, too, shed a few tears, but when Alphonse told her that when the opera house was built there would be a singing spot for her in the shows she was delighted. She said she would be staying with her aunt in Fort Munro until that time.

The last person but one to leave, Madame Lavinsky, received the news coldly. There were no tears or tantrums from her. She carefully wrapped up her crystal ball.

'I can easily get another job,' she told him. 'I can get twice as much as you were paying me.'

Alphonse was relieved that she hadn't become a member of the tearful troupe. There now only remained his wife, Maria. Since he had found out about her infidelity they had hardly spoken. Now he confronted her in their caravan.

'You have ten minutes to pack up your things and leave,' he stated.

'Wh-at? You're throwing me out?'

'What do you expect me to do? Keep a whore under my roof?'

Whereas Alphonse was half-Italian, Marie was half-French. Maybe it was the fact that neither were full-blooded Americans which had attracted them in the first place. There was also the fact that Alphonse's reactions had been assisted by Marie's undoubted attractiveness. She was an olive-skinned, dark-haired beauty and Alphonse had immediately spotted the possibility of using her beauty in his circus. The plan had worked for three years until Marie, irked by the fact that Alphonse was twenty years older than her and an ineffectual lover, had strayed from the narrow path of fidelity. She had found solace in the arms of Nolan. As a result she now found herself pregnant with Nolan's child.

'Where am I going to go?' she wailed.

'You should have thought of that before

you jumped into bed with that gigolo.'

'He wasn't a gigolo. He was a caring man.'

'He didn't care much for you, otherwise he wouldn't have left you,' retorted Alphonse.

Marie bit back the reply which had come unbidden to her lips. She realized that if she was going to have a future which included the everyday luxuries that she was used to she would have to grovel.

'I'll be a dutiful wife from now on. I will look after you as you've never been looked after before. I'll let you do anything you like with me. You can even chain me up and do – whatever you want to do,' she ended hopefully.

'I wouldn't touch you with a bargepole. Look at you, you're already too fat for the skirt you're wearing.'

'I'll help you with your plans to build the opera house.' She was desperate now.

'You've got no part in my plans.'

'Where am I going to go to?' she wailed.

'You can go in the gutter for all I care.'

24

'You bastard.' The wail had turned into a shriek.

'It's you who'll be having the bastard,' chuckled Alphonse.

Marie was not a hot-blooded French woman whose ancestors had come from the Mediterranean region for nothing. She suddenly sprang across the kitchen and before Alphonse could stop her she had opened the drawer of the kitchen table. She grabbed one of the throwing-knives. She spun around and held it aloft menacingly.

'If you're going to kick me out, I'll want some money to take with me. If you don't give me some, I'll stick this in you. It would give me great satisfaction to see you bleeding like the pig you are.' She bared her gums in a triumphant grin.

Alphonse had turned white. He knew this was no idle threat. Marie with a knife in her hand was a dangerous adversary. He knew he would have to give her some money.

'There's fifty dollars in my jacket pocket,' he said, sulkily. 'That's all I've got until I go to the bank.'

Marie backed away towards the jacket which was hanging on a nail. She reached it and groped into one of the pockets. She came up with a bundle of notes and glanced at them briefly.

'This is one hundredth of what you owe me for all I've done for you,' she snapped. 'But it'll have to do for now. If you think for one moment you have heard the last of me, you're making a big mistake.'

With that she flounced out of the caravan.

CHAPTER 4

It was a month later when Ben rode up to the farmhouse. It had an unmistakably deserted air about it. He spurred the horse to arrive more quickly.

He swung out of the saddle before the horse came to a halt.

'Dad,' he shouted as he raced into the house.

Inside his worst fears were confirmed. The place was deserted. It didn't take him two minutes to search the kitchen and sitting-room downstairs, and the two bedrooms upstairs. His search confirmed what he had already guessed – there was no sign of his father.

It was three months since he had visited the farm. In that time anything could have happened. Of course he had intended to come more regularly, but the circus was always too far away. Now, however, he had been sent to Fort Munro by Burke and this gave him the ideal opportunity for a visit. He had been looking forward to meeting his father again, even though his previous visits had generally ended in arguments. But his expectations had been dashed There was nobody at home.

He wondered when was the last time the house had been occupied. A week? A month? Three months? There was no clue in the house. He went outside. The barn was half-stocked up with hay. This could mean something or nothing. Maybe the hay had been there from the last time it had been cut, several months ago. There was no sign of the usual couple of dozen hens which always roamed around the yard. This also could mean something or nothing. Maybe his father had got rid of the hens. Although on second thoughts that was unlikely. The hens provided him with his daily eggs, a couple of which he would usually boil before starting the day's work.

There were no cows either in the field. This was also unusual. The cows provided the milk which his father used to drink and make cheese in the dairy. He went into the dairy. It had the same deserted air as the rest of the farm. The two questions kept hammering at his brain. Where was his father and when did he leave the farm?

There was one possible way of finding out. Dimly he realized that his last month's training as a Pinkerton detective was making him think of eliminating all possibilities until there was one left. Maybe the answer lay there.

He crossed the yard to the well. The well had a rough metal cover to keep the rain out and so provide the inhabitants with clean drinking water. The rain itself was collected in several water butts which were spread out round the farm.

The well-water was the tastiest water he had ever drunk. Due to the depth of the well it was always cold and delicious even in the height of summer. He opened the door and peered inside. His worse fears were realized. The well was almost full, the water reaching just a few inches below the platform on which the bucket rested. Normally, if the well was used regularly for drinking water and for use in cooking the level of the well would be several yards below its present level. All of which indicated that the well hadn't been used for some time. For several weeks probably.

So where were his father and the two hired hands? There was only one way to find out. It meant a visit to Stan Wilkins's farm which he had passed on his way here.

Stan was mending a broken fence when he looked up and saw Ben approaching. He pushed his hat away from his perspiring brow. He was a grizzled fifty-year-old who looked more like seventy. Like his father he had built his farm up from scratch. He kept his gaze steadily on Ben until he was within earshot. Ben noticed that there was no welcoming smile on his grim face.

'Have you heard the news?' Stan greeted him with the question when Ben drew up near him.

'What news, Stan?' Ben feared the worst.

'There's no easy way to tell you this, son. Your father is dead.'

His fears were confirmed. He swung down from his horse.

'How did it happen?'

'He was shot by a stranger.' Stan described how the man who called himself Glen Hillier and who had said he was selling stock for the Wells Railroad Company had first approached him to buy some stock. He told him he wasn't interested in buying any. Hillier had then said he would see whether his neighbour at the next farm would like to buy some.

'Like a fool I told him that Nolan wouldn't be interested either. You see, I gave him your father's name which he might have used as a calling card to get your father's trust.'

'How did he die, Stan?' demanded Ben, evenly.

'I'm coming to that. Some time after Hillier left here I heard a couple of shots coming from the direction of your father's farm. Of course I didn't take any notice of it. I assumed either your father or one of his hired hands were shooting jack rabbits.'

'So Dad was shot?' Ben jumped ahead of Stan's story.

'That's right. The doctor said your father was shot twice in the side of the head. He was on his own in the farm – I didn't know that. The hired hands had gone into Crossville to go to a funeral.'

'When was this, Stan?'

'About six weeks ago. We didn't know where you were to get in touch with you. I saw to all the burial arrangements. You'll find the grave in the cemetery. There's a cross to mark it. I didn't know your father's age so I just put Matthew Nolan. Died eighteen eighty-five.'

'He was just gone fifty,' supplied Ben. 'Thanks for taking care of everything. If you'll let me know the cost of the funeral I'll repay you.'

'There's no need,' said Stan, simply. 'He would have done the same for me.'

Ben's next call was the sheriff's office in Crossville. He knew the sheriff, a large man in his forties who wasn't noted for his quickness of movement or of mind.

Ben explained the purpose of his visit. The sheriff's red face creased in thought.

'I'm sorry about your father. I met him several times when he used to come into market.'

'What about his murderer?' demanded Ben with growing impatience.

'Well, in the first place we don't rightly know that the man who called himself Hillier really was the murderer.'

'He called at my father's farm after calling at Stan Wilkins's farm. About half an hour later Stan heard two shots. How many times was my father shot?'

'Twice.'

'Who found the body?'

'Those two brothers who used to work for

your father, Peter and Paul Drake.'

'I've known Peter and Paul since I was knee-high to a grasshopper. They would never have killed my father, I'd stake my life on it.'

'Maybe somebody else called at the farm between the time that Hillier called there and the brothers found the body,' suggested the sheriff, although without too much conviction.

'How long was that?'

'About three hours.'

'Nobody calls at our farm. It's too far off the beaten track. We could go for months without anybody calling. That's why I left in the end,' Ben ended on a bitter note.

'All right. The chances are that this man, Hillier, killed your father. But he vanished straight afterwards.' The sheriff mopped his face with a large handkerchief. He was looking distinctly uncomfortable under Ben's questioning.

'So what have you done to catch him?'

'I sent a telegram with a description of

34

him to Fort Munro. A couple of days later I had a reply saying that they hadn't seen anyone answering to that description. But they would keep their eyes open.'

Ben stared at him. The sheriff tried to meet his gaze but eventually turned away.

'That's the drawing we had made of him from Stan Wilkins's description.'

Ben went over to the drawing. He saw a man who looked to be in his twenties. He had a rather long face with a thin cruel mouth. He had a fleshy nose which looked as though it had been broken at some time and had not set properly. His eyes were set close together and Ben couldn't see his hair since he was wearing a Stetson.

He stared at the drawing for ages. In fact he stared at it for such a long time that the sheriff coughed to get his attention.

'He's probably miles away by now,' he stated.

'I'll find him,' said Ben, simply. 'When I do, I'll kill him.'

CHAPTER 5

Ben left the sheriff's office and headed for a general store. There he bought a bunch of flowers. Ten minutes later was standing beside his father's grave.

He stared at it for a few moments, his face expressionless. Then he pulled out the wooden cross with the inscription on it. He took out a penknife and added Born 1835 before pushing the cross back in.

He stood over the grave for ages. His mind went back to the happy moments before his mother had died of influenza. After that his relationship with his father soured. He had been fourteen at the time. He had worked on the farm for several years before he made the decisive break. It had been a huge relief to him when he had taken the decision. In a strange way he had felt that it had also been a relief to his father, even though he had been left to run the farm with just two hired men.

There was nobody in the churchyard to watch the still figure. At last Ben whispered:

'I'll get the bastard that killed you, if it's the last thing I do.' He took one last look at the grave and this time a tear ran down his face.

His next call was a saloon. He ordered a whiskey. There were about a dozen men in the bar. He went over his promise to his father to find Hillier. Maybe the fact that he was working for the Pinkerton agency might come in useful. They had a string of agents across America. When he got back to the office he could use them by sending telegrams. There were always wanted men whom the agency advertised for in this way. Not only that but if Hillier was selling bogus railway stock then Pinkerton's themselves could be eager to catch him. Their priority had always been the railways, and any criminal activity associated with that growing form of transport was always given priority.

Half an hour later he was on his fifth whiskey, or was it his sixth? Normally he wasn't a drinking man. In fact when he was working in Alphonse's circus he hardly ever took a drink. It was necessary that he had a steady hand to throw the knives and so the last thing he wanted was a hangover which could mean a shaky hand, which could have put Marie's life in danger.

It took him a few moments to realize that the man standing next to him was asking him if he wanted a drink. Normally he would have accepted. It would have meant getting into conversation with the stranger, but there was nothing wrong with that. He was a gregarious type who would generally speak to 'most anyone. However this time he hesitated.

'Did you hear what I said? Can I buy you a drink?' asked the stranger.

Ben hadn't taken much notice of him until then, now he studied him. He looked something like the drawing of Hillier, he had the thin long face with eyes set close together. Whereas Hillier had been clean-shaven, the stranger had a full moustache. There was no way he could have grown the moustache in the few weeks since his father had died.

'Well, are you going to have a drink or not?' This time there was belligerence in the stranger's tone.

'No, thanks,' said Ben, turning away.

'Nobody refuses Silas Caldy when I offer to buy them a drink.' The stranger had raised his voice. It silenced several of those standing nearby.

'I said, no.' Ben still had his back to him.

Caldy hit Ben hard in the back.

'Nobody turns their back on me when I'm talking to them either.'

This time Ben did turn. His quick glance took in the two guns in Caldy's holster.

'Do you want to make something of it?' Ben didn't know why he uttered the remark. Normally if there was any threat of danger he would walk away from it. His father had told him enough tales of the Civil War and the way men had behaved like animals during that time to make him want to avoid any conflict. Even though his father had brought him up to despise war and anything to do with it, he had insisted on him learning to draw a gun quickly. That was why he had impressed Burke and Grey when he had applied for the position in Pinkerton's.

'If you say so, mister.'

Caldy had sidled further along the bar so that they were now several yards apart.

The bar had gone strangely silent. The barman had quickly removed the bottle of whiskey and shoved it below the counter. He himself had prepared to duck down behind it if any shooting started.

Ben stared at Caldy who had now moved so that there was about twenty feet between them.

'I'm asking you for the last time,' he growled. 'Do you want a drink?'

'And I'm telling you for the last time, no,' replied Ben, evenly.

'Nobody refuses me when I offer to buy

them a drink,' Caldy reiterated, belligerently.

Ben was busy calculating the distance between them. It would be about seven yards. He knew that if Caldy drew his gun first he would be joining his father in Boot Hill, since his opponent couldn't possibly fail at that distance. So he had to make sure that he drew first.

Caldy hesitated. Maybe that was a sign he was going to call it off. Both had their right hands poised above their guns. Nobody broke the silence. The only sound to be heard was the tick tock of the grandfather clock behind the bar. It was strange but normally nobody would ever hear the clock – there was usually too much noise going on. But now the clock was noisily ticking the seconds away.

Suddenly Caldy went for his gun. Ben drew his with startling rapidity. He knew even before he fired that he had won the draw.

CHAPTER 6

In the Pinkerton office Burke was studying a telegram. He read it for the second time then reread it again. Then he summoned Grey. When he arrived he showed him the telegram. Grey read it then gave a low whistle. Burke waited for him to make a comment. When it came it was:

'I always thought there was something unsavoury about that character.'

'The question is, what are we going to do about it?' demanded Burke.

'We could ignore it,' suggested Grey, hopefully. 'After all, if Nolan goes around getting involved in a gunfight with a stranger, then it's nothing to do with us.'

'The sheriff of Crossville sent us this.' Burke tapped the telegram with the back of his hand. 'It would be discourteous not to reply to it.'

Grey shifted his ground. 'Well we could just confirm that Nolan is one of our employees. And add that he has only been working for us for a few weeks, so we really don't know much about him.'

Burke read the telegram again as though it might help him to make up his mind about the reply. It read:

TO THE PINKERTON AGENCY, CHICAGO.

I HAVE A PRISONER IN CUSTODY WHO SHOT A STRANGER IN A SALOON. HE IS TO BE TRIED ON FRIDAY. HE SAYS HE WORKS FOR YOU. COULD YOU CONFIRM THIS AND LET ME HAVE ANY INFORM-ATION ABOUT HIM THAT YOU MIGHT HAVE.

THE SHERIFF OF CROSSVILLE.

'Nolan must have had a good reason to shoot this guy,' remarked Burke, half to himself. 'He didn't seem the sort of person who would act without a good reason.'

'He was a fornicator,' said Grey. 'I never trusted him.'

Burke ignored the comment. 'I know he was only working for us for a few weeks, but there was nothing wrong with his work. He played his part when the New York train was attacked by outlaws.'

'They say he killed one of the bandits, maybe he got a taste for killing,' said Grey, drily.

Burke came to a decision. 'Anyhow he's one of us. We've always prided ourselves on looking after our own. The least we can do is to give him a good reference.'

'So you're going to send a telegram back,' suggested Grey.

'No, I'm going to send you back,' said Burke. 'I want you to stay there until the trial. See that he has a fair hearing. Point out that he was a satisfactory employee.'

Ben was languishing in Crossville jail. It was not a situation which he relished. He had assumed that, after going to the sheriff and confessing that he had killed a man in the saloon who had instigated a fight, then he would be discharged. After all he had several witnesses who could testify that Caldy had been annoying Ben with his persistent demands to buy him a drink. On top of this one of the witnesses knew Caldy personally and was able to vouch that he was a trouble-maker. He had been responsible for several fist fights in other saloons. In fact he had been banned from several saloons in the town, which was why he had happened to be in the same saloon as Ben.

A couple of witnesses had been rounded up by the deputy sheriff the day after the shooting. Ben hadn't objected to spending one night in the cells – he had expected that. But he had expected also that after the sheriff had collected the witnesses' statements then he would be released. But a big shock awaited him. The sheriff had charged Ben with murder, and had fixed his trial for the end of the following week. In the meantime he was to stay in jail.

Ben slowly came to terms with the fact that things weren't as straightforward as they had appeared. He would have to spend another ten days in jail. He had never been in jail before. Indeed if his father were alive he would have been horrified to learn that Ben was in jail. The family prided themselves in not breaking the law. His forefathers had been strict churchgoers, even though Ben himself wasn't a regular attender and going to church equated staying out of jail.

The cell was twenty feet by fifteen. Once he had ascertained that fact, there seemed nothing else to do. He knew that the deputy sheriff, a spotty-faced young man named Hanklin, was seated in the small room beyond, indeed Ben derived some small satisfaction in the knowledge that his cell was bigger than Hanklin's room. Then beyond that was the sheriff's office. And beyond that again was the main street and freedom. A freedom for which he would have to wait another ten days before he could go out and savour it.

CHAPTER 7

If Grey had been a swearing man he would have let forth a string of expletives. The fact that he was going to Fort Munro and then on to Crossville to give a reference to a man he disliked was like fire on his skin. If Nolan was an ordinary churchgoing citizen he would have been pleased to travel the considerable distance to Crossville to give him support. But Nolan was a self-confessed adulterer. On top of that he hadn't shown any remorse about his actions.

So here he was in an uncomfortable carriage on his way to Fort Munro. It would mean that he would be spending several days away from his wife and family. It would mean that his wife, Ruth, would have to look after their seven children on her own. True, her sister, Margaret, would be calling in from time to time, but apart from taking and fetching the children from the church school, she wouldn't provide any help. So Ruth would have to manage on her own for the next week or so. And all because that adulterer had become involved in a gunfight.

It wasn't as if he could do anything positive about the situation when he arrived in Crossville. He knew nothing about Nolan's past, except what the son of Sodom and Gomorra had divulged. All he would be able to say was that Nolan was an employee of Pinkerton's who had worked for them for only a few weeks. That would hardly make any difference to any trial. The probability was that Nolan had shot somebody in a saloon in self-defence and he was going to be released after the formalities of trial had been observed. And here he was being forced to suffer by sitting on a hard train seat for hours. He put a boiled sweet in his mouth. It would help to provide him with some slight comfort for the next few minutes.

Ben was surprised when, on his third day in captivity, the deputy came in and announced that he was going to have a visitor.

'Who is it?' Ben demanded.

The deputy surprised him by announcing it was a young lady.

'Show her in,' said Ben.

The deputy ushered her in, at the same time bringing in a chair for her.

'Thank you,' she said, rewarding the deputy with a winning smile.

Ben regarded her. She was a pretty young thing. He didn't know why he assumed she was young, except that she had a certain innocent air about her. She had a pretty face and the sort of lovely blue eyes that a man could spend ages looking into. He shook his head to try to clear his thoughts. Any desires about a woman were the last things he needed. If Marie hadn't tempted him to share her bed he would still be working at Alphonse's circus and so he wouldn't be in the mess he now found himself in.

She had taken off her bonnet. She shook her blonde curls. In spite of his initial response not to become involved with a woman Ben still couldn't take his eyes off her.

'I think I'd better introduce myself. I'm Sylvia Sanderson. I visit people who are in jail. And the sick,' she added, as an afterthought.

'I'm Ben Nolan.' They shook hands formally.

She regarded him with her large blue eyes. Ben returned her stare.

Eventually she said, 'You don't look like a gunslinger.'

'I'm not a gunslinger,' Ben protested. 'I just got into an argument in a saloon. I was forced to draw to save my life.'

'Saloons are dens of iniquity,' she said, reproachfully.

'I suppose that's one way of looking at them.'

'It's the only way,' she said, with surprising vehemence.

'I'm not going to argue with you,' said Ben, dismissively.

'What's the matter, are you afraid of hearing the truth?' She leaned forward in her chair.

He was sitting on the bed and couldn't help but notice that not only did she have a pretty face, but she had a nice figure too.

'There are two things I never argue about. Religion and politics.'

'Religion is the only thing worth arguing about,' she said with passion. 'My father's a minister,' she announced as an afterthought.

'I see.'

'You think I'm here to try to convert you to Christianity, don't you, Mr Nolan.'

'Call me Ben.'

'But I'm not an evangelist. I just believe in helping people who are in trouble.'

'How old are you?'

'I don't see that it's any of your business,' she snapped. Then she relented. 'I'm seventeen, going on eighteen.'

'Well, Sylvia, I'm sorry to disappoint you,

but I'm not in trouble. They're just keeping me here as a formality before they try me and then release me on Friday.'

She seemed uncertain for the first time since entering his cell. The low sun came through the barred window and caught her golden curls. She stared at him with slightly parted lips. Whether it was her nearness or whether he had seen a fleeting expression on her face he would never know.

However he stood up, moved close to her, and kissed her on those perfect lips. If his action was unexpected her reaction was equally surprising. She sat motionless for a long while, letting him kiss her. Then when he eventually drew away she stood up.

He looked at her narrowed eyes and look of hatred. Her next move was quite predictable. She slapped him hard on the face.

CHAPTER 8

Grey arrived in Crossville on the day before the trial. He booked in at what appeared to be the best saloon in town. It was called the Antelope. Grey observed critically that the service did not live up to the name on the billboard since it was ten minutes before anyone appeared in answer to his hitting the bell on the counter.

'Sorry about that,' said a burly shirt-sleeved figure who gave the distinct impression that he had just got out of bed.

'I'd like a room for the night,' said Grey.

'Have you come for the trial?' demanded the other.

Grey was surprised by the question but was saved from having to answer by the appearance of an equally burly woman. Grey who, as a detective, was used to adding two and two together this time didn't even have to go as far as that in deducing that they had been in bed together when he had rung the bell.

'Bill, take the gentleman's bag to his room,' said the woman. When Bill had disappeared with Grey's case she presented the register for Grey to sign.

'Your husband said something about a trial,' he stated, as he signed.

'It's tomorrow. They're trying a man who shot somebody in a saloon. Not this saloon,' she added with a smile, showing rotten teeth.

Grey smiled, dutifully. He supposed that a trial, any trial was a big event in a small town like this. He decided to find out more about Nolan's shoot-out; after all, the telegram hadn't told them much.

'What exactly happened?' he demanded, casually.

'Well, I've heard several reports.' She folded her arms over her ample bosom. 'But the most reliable one came from one of our own customers, Percy Lightfoot. He said that Nolan – that's the name of the accused – deliberately riled Silas Caldy. Of course that's easy to imagine. Caldy was a regular hothead. In fact he'd been banned from most saloons in town, including this one.'

'So it was a fair fight in the saloon?' probed Grey.

'If you can call any fight a fair fight.' The landlady sniffed disapprovingly. 'It seems that Caldy didn't stand a chance. They say that the speed with which Nolan drew his gun had to be seen to be believed.'

Grey could vouch for that. He had seen Nolan give a demonstration of his expertise with a gun in Burke's office. He had seen some fast draws in his twenty years with the agency, but Nolan was up there with the best.

'I suppose the result of the trial will be a foregone conclusion,' he ventured.

'Well, knowing Caldy's reputation as a hothead, you're probably right. But the judge is Judge Pearson, and he's against all kinds of firearms.'

Grey mulled over the landlady's remark as he went up to his room to unpack. If the judge was against all kinds of firearms then maybe the case against Nolan wasn't cut and dried after all. Maybe the judge would give him a nominal sentence – say a few weeks. If he did it would be the end of his career in Pinkerton's. It was one of the agency's rules that they did not employ criminals. Nolan would be classed as a criminal even if he only served a month in jail. It would be enough to blacken his name. It would mean that he would no longer be an employee of Pinkerton's.

And good riddance too. Grey almost smiled at the thought as he started to unpack his clothes. He had never liked the man. Nolan was too smooth by far – a ladies' man. He was the sort of man who could pick and choose which lady to make love to. And they would fall at his feet, there was no doubt about that. He himself had only had one woman in his life – his wife. Not that he ever regretted having had only one woman, of course. They were happily married and he was devoted to his wife and his seven children. But now and again somebody like Nolan came along. Somebody who was better-looking than most men. Somebody who was too confident in his own ability. Somebody who could draw a gun with lightning speed. Somebody who had obviously had lots of women. Somebody whom it was very easy to dislike – hate even.

He finished unpacking. Tomorrow could prove to be an interesting day. Until now he had assumed that the whole tedious journey would be a waste of time. That all he would have to do would be to stand in the witness box and confirm that Nolan had worked for the agency for a few weeks. But the fact that Judge Pearson, who was against all firearms, was the judge, might make the trial more interesting than he had anticipated.

CHAPTER 9

The trial in fact started as a low-key affair. True, all the seats in the converted school-room were full. True, there was some slight difficulty in swearing in the jury, since one of them, Joshua Starling, had stated that he could only leave his farm for an hour at the most since one of his cows was due to calve, and if the trial went on longer than that, he would have to leave. Judge Pearson, a short, stern-faced grey-haired man, took umbrage at the remark. He reminded Starling that this was a court of law and as such took precedence over his cows. This caused a slight ripple of laughter among the on-lookers.

There was also a stir when Ben was led in. He was handcuffed, although he had argued with the deputy that there was no need for such treatment – he obviously wasn't going to run away. The deputy merely ignored his remark and finished putting the cuffs on him.

The judge banged his gavel on the desk to restore order. Ben was led to a makeshift dock in the front corner of the hall. Ben, who had never been in a court of law before, studied the spectators interestedly. The only person he recognized was Grey, who was sitting in the back row. Well, at least if there was any doubt about his innocence, Grey would be able to set the record straight that he was an upright member of society.

At that moment there was a new arrival – two, in fact. Ben immediately recognized the first as Sylvia Sanderson. The person with her, who was wearing a dog-collar, Ben guessed was her father. Some of the people sitting on the bench moved up to make room for them. Ben hadn't taken his eyes off Sylvia, but she had studiously refrained from looking in his direction. Maybe she didn't want to recognize him now that he was wearing handcuffs. His mind went back to the moment in the cell when he had kissed her. It had been a spur of the moment impulse. Maybe it had been prompted by the fact that he had been kept more or less in isolation for three days. Maybe it had been prompted by her nearness and above all by the fact that she was so pretty. Whatever mixed reasons there were for his impulsive action, he did not regret it. He did not even regret the slap which had followed it – he had been slapped by ladies before. One thing he was prepared to swear though – although she had remained impassive when he had kissed her there had just been a couple of seconds at the end when she had started to respond. The moments had been brief but he would have sworn that it had happened.

The clerk was now insisting on a different type of swearing – he was holding a Bible towards Ben.

'Place your right hand on the Bible and

swear to tell the truth,' the clerk, a thin man with a lugubrious creased face, prompted.

Ben held his hands showing that it was difficult to place his right hand on the Bible. The judge intervened.

'Take the cuffs off him,' he ordered. 'Who was it who put them on him in the first place?'

The deputy shuffled apologetically forward. Ben couldn't resist a smirk of satisfaction when he removed the handcuffs.

Ben duly swore on the Bible and the trial began. Ben confirmed his name. He also confirmed that he had shot Silas Caldy.

'I was a fair fight,' he added. 'There are witnesses who can vouch that he was trying to pick a fight.' Ben had now recognized two of the men who had been in the bar at the time.

'So you admit that you killed Caldy,' said the judge, slowly. 'Have you ever killed a man before?'

'No, your honour,' replied Ben.

'Would you say that up until that moment

you had been a god-fearing, respectable citizen?'

Ben didn't like the god-fearing part. He had never been very strong on religion. His mother used to go to church regularly before she was suddenly taken ill. The fact that she had been god-fearing hadn't helped her in the end. She had contracted the infection and had died within a week.

'Well?' the judge was waiting impatiently for an answer.

Well, he certainly qualified for one part of the question – he had definitely been a respectable citizen. He replied, 'Yes, your honour.'

The judge's next question was whether he had any witnesses who could confirm Ben's claim. The obvious person was Grey. Ben informed the judge, who called him to take the stand.

After Grey had been sworn in, the judge asked him whether he could confirm Ben's assertion that he was an upright citizen. Grey hesitated. Ben felt mildly annoyed.

After all, it was a straightforward question, all Grey had to do was to stand up for him.

He couldn't believe what he was hearing. Grey was stating that he didn't know anything about Ben's past – they had accepted him as an agent for Pinkerton's without any references since they were short of men. In fact, in normal circumstances they wouldn't have employed Ben.

'Why not?' The judge leaned forward interestedly.

'Well, he admitted to having had an affair with a married woman. Normally that would have meant that he would not have been offered a post with the agency. But as I've said, we're short of suitable men.'

Ben's anger had reached boiling point on hearing Grey's assessment.

'Wasn't I a satisfactory employee when I was working for Pinkerton's?' He had raised his voice.

'There's no need to shout, Mr Nolan. We will conduct this trial like civilized human beings,' said the judge. 'Answer the question.' He addressed the remark to Grey.

'Well, it's difficult to say,' replied Grey, calmly. 'Nolan had only been working for us for a few weeks. We really hadn't had time to form an opinion about him.'

'All right, you can step down,' said the judge. As an afterthought he added, 'Unless you've any more questions?'

'No,' replied Ben, wearily.

The judge looked at his notes.

'I would like to call Stan Wilkins.'

Wilkins stepped forward. Ben heaved a sigh of relief. After Grey's not very helpful evidence he was sure that Stan would find something to say in his favour.

'I understand you have something to contribute to the case,' said the judge.

Wilkins took the stand. He appeared to be nervous. He took the oath and began:

'Ben's father died a few weeks ago. Ben came back to find that his father was dead. In fact he had been shot by a man named Hillier. He said he was a representative of Wells Railroad Company. He wheedled his way into Ben's father's house. Then he shot him. When Ben came back he found that his father had been killed.'

Some of those in the schoolroom began to look sympathetically at Ben. Until now they had regarded him largely with suspicion, which was reinforced by the fact that Ben had been led in with handcuffs on. But now it was obvious that many had suddenly formed a more sympathetic opinion of the accused. Particularly the women who couldn't kelp noticing that beneath the several days' growth of beard there was a quite handsome man.

The judge thanked Wilkins for his evidence. He asked Ben whether he had anything to add. Ben replied that he hadn't. The judge appealed for any more witnesses from those in court.

One of the men who had been in the bar when the shooting had taken place came forward. He took the oath and was obviously pleased to have become the sudden centre of attention. He stated that his name was Dan

Minton. He confirmed that he had seen the whole episode. He described in graphic detail how Caldy had kept on trying to buy the accused a drink, but he had refused. In the end Caldy had moved down the bar.

'It was obvious there was going to be a fight,' Minton concluded.

'In your opinion who was responsible for the fight?' demanded the judge.

'There's only one answer to that,' replied Minton. 'It was Silas of course. He'd always been a nuisance ever since I knew him.'

'There's a difference between being a nuisance and challenging a person to a gun-fight,' said the judge, drily. 'Had you ever seen this man Caldy involved in a gunfight before?'

Minter confessed that he hadn't.

'So presumably part of the blame was on the accused. If he had accepted the drink that Caldy had offered to buy him, then probably there would have been no gunfight?'

'Probably,' agreed Minton.

What was the judge trying to do? Was he

trying to prove that somehow he was partly responsible for the gunfight? Minton had shown in his evidence that Caldy had been a regular nuisance. If Caldy hadn't approached him in the first place then he would have continued having a quiet drink. Eventually he would have left the saloon. And that would have been that. But Caldy had had to butt in. In the end it was Caldy who had challenged him to a gunfight by taking up his position several yards away.

The judge finally called him to the stand. Ben explained exactly what had happened. With the explanation came a growing sense that the jury would be bound to accept his explanation.

There was a lengthy pause. The judge coughed. It was obviously a preliminary to his summing-up, when there was a sudden stir in the back row. The minister who had come in with Sylvia Sanderson stood up.

'I've got something to add which concerns this case,' he stated.

All eyes focused on him, not least Ben's.

What could he possibly have to contribute? He hadn't been in the saloon, had he, when the gunfight took place?

The judge, too, gave him his full attention. 'What do you think you can contribute, Paul?'

So the judge and the minister were on first-name terms. Well, that wasn't so strange. After all, they were both pillars of the community. Ben's gaze had now switched to Sylvia. She was sitting bolt upright with her eyes fixed on some point on the ceiling. For the first time a tiny measure of doubt surfaced in his mind. It seemed as though she was deliberately refraining from looking in his direction. Did that mean something? Or nothing? He had read somewhere that in a court of law when a jury returns in a murder trial and they refuse to look at the accused it means that they have found him guilty.

Ben shook his head slightly to banish such wayward thoughts. The minister began to speak.

'What I have to say is not very pleasant,' he began. What on earth can it be? Ben wondered. He found out when the minister uttered his next sentence. 'The accused assaulted my daughter when she came to visit him in jail.'

To say that there was an audible gasp from those present would be an understatement. The noise level almost approached the warning blast of a river boat's hooter.

'It's a lie.' Ben's voice could be heard above the noise. The judge banged his gavel.

'I must have silence in court.'

Ben was still shouting. The vicar was still on his feet. The judge was still banging his instrument.

'If you don't shut up,' he shouted at Ben, 'I'll give you a month's jail for contempt of court.'

The threat was enough to quieten Ben. He had already spent nearly a fortnight in jail. The last thing he wanted was another month.

'We'll hear what the lady herself has to

say,' said the judge. 'Will you please take the stand.'

Sylvia came forward reluctantly. Indeed, before setting out she had an argument with her father in hushed tones. From her attitude it appeared that she did not want to give evidence. Her father propelled her along the aisle. Even then she turned imploringly towards him as though beseeching him to let her stay in her seat.

'I'm waiting, young lady,' said the judge, not too unkindly.

Due to the fact that most of the school-room had been taken up by the benches, there was very little space at the front. Ben was standing in one corner with the judge seated at a desk at the back. Sylvia was forced to stand near to Ben while the clerk presented her with the Bible and read out the oath.

Once again Ben was struck by the fact that she looked so attractive, even though her face was drawn and her eyes were glazed. However when she began to give her evidence she did so in a clear, confident voice.

She described how she had visited Ben in jail. She said they had had a short meeting, then at the end of it something had happened. There was an expectant silence from the listeners. 'He seized me and forced me to endure him kissing me.'

For the first time she looked directly at him. Whereas before there had been some diffidence in her stance there was now a hint of triumph in her attitude.

The judge had to bang several times to quell the excited buzz which greeted her revelation.

'Do you wish to question the witness?' he asked Ben.

He hesitated. She was now standing staring at him. He felt that she was daring him to contradict her statement. At last he said, 'It was only a kiss. She slapped my face. I deserved it. I would now like to publicly apologize for my behaviour.'

'Right, that will be all.' The judge

addressed the remark to Sylvia. She flushed, turned on her heel and flounced back to her seat.

The judge began his summing up. He stated that apparently Nolan had killed Caldy in a fair gunfight. However it didn't excuse the fact that Nolan could apparently have walked away from the fight at any time.

'In this town we pride ourselves on being law abiding citizens. We do not condone the use of guns. Whereas Nolan's behaviour might have been acceptable in other parts of the country, here it is definitely not to be condoned. I feel, however, that I must take into account that the accused had just heard about his father's death. This could have affected him in some respect. In fact it is due to that extenuating circumstance that I'm going to reduce the original sentence which I would have given him. The reduced sentence is now two years' hard labour.'

The collective gasp from the audience outdid anything which had come before. The look of disbelief was frozen on Ben's face. It was only broken when there was a sudden commotion from the back of the schoolroom. Sylvia had fainted.

CHAPTER 10

'I must say I'm surprised,' said Burke.

Grey had returned to Chicago with the news. Strangely enough the journey back to the town had been far less tedious as far as he was concerned than when he had travelled to Crossville. On the occasions when he had found it becoming boring Grey had only to imagine the expression on Nolan's face when he had received the sentence. At the thought he would smile to himself. Indeed he was in danger of appearing to be some sort of idiot in the eyes of fellow-passengers on the train, who began to regard him as somebody who often smiled to himself for no reason at all.

'It's a very strict town,' supplied Grey. 'They don't like guns. Also there was the business of the minister's daughter.'

'What was that about?' demanded Burke, with increased interest.

'Well, apparently Nolan assaulted her when she went to visit him in jail?'

'Assaulted her in jail?' Burke's voice rose.

'That's what she said. He didn't deny it either.'

Burke shook his head in disbelief. Grey deliberately didn't elaborate by telling him that Nolan had actually only kissed her.

'I never did trust him.' Grey couldn't keep the gloating out of his tones.

'To assault the minister's daughter...' Burke again shook his head.

'Shall I get rid of his file?' Grey demanded, eagerly.

'Well he certainly won't be coming back here,' stated Burke, as though he had just made an important decision.

In Fort Munro Alphonse was meeting the town committee. This was the third time he had met them in as many weeks. Whereas the previous meetings had been preliminary fact-finding ones, this was now the make-or-break meeting. Alphonse knew that if the powerful and rich members of the committee did not come up with the money to build the opera house then his whole dream would be shattered. There would be no opera house.

Originally there had been six members of the committee, but when they had discovered that they themselves would be expected to contribute to the cost of the opera house the number had suddenly changed to four. These four were Graveney, a bank manager, Rawlings, who owned several saloons, Blake, who was obviously rich but whose source of income wasn't too apparent, and Stone, a wealthy farmer.

The meeting was taking place in the lounge of one of Rawlings's saloons. Having seen that they had full glasses Rawlings retired into the background, handing over the reins of control to Graveney, the bank manager.

Graveney coughed to indicate that the meeting was now open.

'Since the last meeting, Mr Carvello, we have had another discussion among ourselves. There still a few unresolved questions which we would like you to clear up.'

Alphonse waited expectantly. He could hazard a guess at what those questions were.

'In the first place,' continued Graveney, 'we would like to know exactly what kind of entertainment you intend putting on in your opera house. Of course we've all heard of Mozart's operas, but what other operas have you in mind?'

'Mozart was a German,' said Alphonse, dismissively. 'I intend bringing Italian operas. The operas of the great Italian composers like Verdi, Rossini and Puccini.'

That's all very laudable,' continued Graveney. 'But I would assume that these would be more suitable in a city like New York, where they have an audience who are more educated in listening to classical music.'

'I intend to make Fort Munro a second New York,' said Alphonse, passionately.

'It's the wrong type of community,' said

Blake, dismissively. 'I'm all for building an opera house, but it must appeal to all. There must be plays here, light entertainment, circuses even.'

Alphonse was going to argue when he suddenly saw that it would be better to go along with that idiot Blake's suggestion. Once the opera house had been built then he would be in charge. He would be the one who would decide what kind of entertainment would be put on.

'Yes, that sounds reasonable,' he conceded.

'Right, that's settled,' said Graveney. 'It only remains to decide how much each of us is willing to contribute towards the project. I'll start the ball rolling by stating that the bank will advance five thousand dollars.'

Privately Alphonse was hoping for double that amount, but he held his peace.

'I'll put in the same,' said Rawlings.

'Me, too,' said Stone.

If Alphonse had expected Blake to balk at the sums so far donated, he was mistaken.

'And me,' said Blake, casually.

The others were now looking at Alphonse. He felt like the captain of a yacht who suddenly finds the guns of an enemy frigate trained on him.

'I'm not a wealthy man,' he began in some confusion.

'How much?' asked Blake, who had suddenly assumed a more purposeful role.

'One thousand dollars. Of course I'll be bringing along all my expertise,' he added quickly.

'You ran a circus, I believe,' said Stone, drily.

'Yes, that's right,' conceded Alphonse. Why was he sweating?

'Has anyone got anything else to say?' demanded Graveney. Nobody stirred. 'Right, it seems satisfactory,' he said to Alphonse's huge relief. 'I'll arrange for a solicitor to draw up the agreement. We'll meet again in a few days' time. The sooner this project gets off the ground the better.'

CHAPTER 11

Ben had worked on the chaingang for six months and every day had cursed the impulse which had made him fight Caldy. He also cursed the overseer, a burly man named Stevens who was overzealous with his whip. He cursed the judge for not being more lenient with his sentencing. For good measure he cursed Grey for not giving him a more positive character reference.

The gang were working on a railway. Ironically it was the railway leading to Fort Munro from Crossville. It was believed that the building of the railway would bring added prosperity to Crossville. The sooner that prosperity came the better, was the argument. Which was why Ben and the other members of the chaingang had to work eight hours a day to make sure the railway was completed on time.

Those working in the chaingang were unchained for half an hour during the middle of the day. That was the time when they ate their meagre rations and drank their sparse allowance of water. Ben's neighbour, a Negro named Horace, informed Ben that they were lucky to be unchained for half an hour. On the last chain-gang on which he had worked they had been chained up for the whole eight hours.

At first Ben wasn't eager to get into conversation with Horace. For the first few weeks Ben was too disgusted with the situation in which he found himself to speak to anyone. Ben regarded himself as the lowest of the low: a sub-human species forced to work in appalling conditions, his life ruled over by Stevens's whip. Gradually, however, he relented. He began to talk to Horace during their lunch break.

Horace accepted the change in Ben's attitude magnanimously.

'That's it, man. You've got to talk sometime. We all felt the same way as you the first time we were chained up. What are you here for?'

Ben explained how he shot a man in a saloon fight.

'You say it was a fair fight,' demanded Horace, incredulously. 'Then why were you sentenced to two years on the chaingang?'

'The judge didn't like me. One of the reasons was that I kissed the minister's daughter when she came to visit me in jail.'

'Was she your girlfriend?' demanded Horace.

'No, I'd never met her before,' confessed Ben. Horace stared at Ben. Then his face split in a wide grin. 'Man, you're something else,' he chortled.

'What about you?' demanded Ben. 'Why are you here?'

'They say I raped a white woman,' replied Horace.

'And did you?'

'No, man. I was working on their ranch. Her name was Gloria. She was the owner's wife. She was as pretty as a picture.'

He fell silent as though contemplating just how pretty a picture she had been.

'What happened?' prompted Ben.

'Well, we had all been working in the fields. I was helping to cut the corn and stack it. Suddenly my scythe slipped. Instead of cutting the corn, I cut my finger. The foreman told me to go back to the ranch to get my finger bandaged. I ran back to the ranch. When I got there Gloria set about bandaging my finger.' He sighed. 'She was as pretty as a picture.'

'So you've said. What happened next?'

'When she had finished she said maybe I should lie down to recover. I said I was all right, but she insisted. So I lain down on the sofa. The next thing she had lain down beside me. I knew what she wanted. But I swear I didn't touch her. But when she heard one of the men coming in she ripped her dress. Then she swore that I'd raped her.'

There was a lengthy pause. At last Ben said:

'So they sentenced you to the chaingang. For how many years?'

'Seven. But I'm not staying here much longer, Ben. I'm going to escape in a few days' time.'

'Do you know what you're saying?' They were whispering now. 'The guards will have shot you before you will have gone fifty yards.'

'I've got it all planned,' whispered Horace, urgently. 'I'll do it when it starts raining. The guards and Stevens all stay in their tent when it's raining. They think that nobody has tried to escape up till now, and so nobody will be brave enough to try it.'

'Foolish enough, you mean,' said Ben, sharply.

'See that wood,' said Horace, pointing to a wood about 300 yards away.

'Yep,' Ben surveyed it, thoughtfully.

'Well, we're at the nearest point to it now. We've been gradually getting closer to it during these past few weeks. If I don't take my chance shortly, we'll be moving further away from it. Then I'd be stuck in this chaingang for another five years,' he ended bitterly.

Ben thought over Horace's decision during the rest of the day. It was a foolish one. Common sense said that Horace would never reach the wood before the guards realized that he was trying to escape and shot him. Even if Horace managed to reach the wood he would be wearing the distinctive clothing of a convict. As soon as somebody spotted him he would be tied down and eventually caught again. When he was returned to the chain gang he would be publicly whipped to within an inch of life. That was the punishment. All the others in the chaingang would be forced to watch as a deterrent to their ever trying to escape.

He decided to impress on Horace the foolishness of his decision the next morning. However when the day dawned it was accompanied by a persistent heavy rain. One look at Horace's smiling face told Ben all he wished to know. Horace would be making his bid for freedom if the rain persisted until the morning break.

In fact, if anything the rain became more persistent. Ben found himself involuntarily glancing at the sky every few minutes to see whether there was any sign of the rain abating. There was none.

At last the time for their morning break arrived. Stevens hurriedly came down the line, unlocking each convict as quickly as he could. He didn't look at their faces, such was his hurry to get the job finished and go back to the tent where he would enjoy a hot meal. If he had looked at Horace's face he might have been struck by the fact that the Negro was smiling, even in such atrocious weather conditions.

Horace watched until Stevens had unlocked everyone and had returned hurriedly to the tent. He turned to Ben.

'Wish me luck,' he said.

'I'm coming with you,' Ben heard himself say.

Horace's smile grew even bigger.

'Right, man, let's go,' he said.

They stood up. A few of the prisoners who were seated nearby looked at them with puzzlement. Normally when one of the prisoners stood up there would be a loud shout for them to sit down. If they didn't obey with alacrity then Stevens's whip would gave them a sharp reminder not to disobey in the future.

However Stevens and the guards were in the tent. True, one of them would put his head out every few seconds. But in that time Horace and Ben were hoping to reach the safety of the trees.

The two were running like the wind. Months of hard exercise in the chaingang had hardened Ben's muscles and he knew he was running towards the trees faster than he had ever run in his life. At any moment, though, they expected to hear a shout from behind them. But every second the trees were getting invitingly nearer. They had now covered half the distance towards safety. Whereas when he had started Ben was breathing relatively smoothly, now his breath was coming in huge gasps. He knew he was slowing down. A quick glance to his right told him that Horace was also suffering. We started off too quickly, was Ben's last thought before there was the sound of gunfire. A couple of bullets sped past uncomfortably close to them.

For a brief moment Ben thought about zigzagging to try to put the guards off their aim. He rejected the idea as soon as it came. If they wasted time zigzagging it would mean that it would take them longer to reach the trees.

The bullets were peppering the ground around them. Suddenly Horace gave a yell of pain.

'Have you been hit?' cried Ben, glancing at him with concern.

'It's only a scratch,' Horace replied.

Ben's relief was short-lived. A bullet came so close to his hair that he involuntarily put his hand to his head to see whether he too, had been hit. No, but it had been a close thing. Too close for comfort.

The trees were now only about fifty yards away.

'We're almost there,' yelled Horace, exultantly.

Don't tempt fate, pleaded Ben inwardly. Please don't tempt fate. His chest heaved as he pushed his legs to make one last effort to reach the trees. Fifty yards. Thirty yards. Ten yards. One of the bullets actually hit the tree in front of him. Then came Horace's next shout.

'We've made it, man!'

They were both hanging on to their nearest tree, trying to get their breath back. Even as he did so Ben was busy calculating how much of an advantage they had over their pursuers. If the guards were already following them then they had five minutes' grace at the most.

'Come on,' he said, urgently. 'Let's go.'

'Which way?' demanded Horace.

'This way,' said Ben, sharply.

'How do you know?'

'Because I used to live not far from here,' retorted Ben.

'Well I'll be damned,' said Horace.

CHAPTER 12

Ben knew roughly in which direction his farm lay. If his calculations were correct it was about five miles due south. He began to lead the way with Horace following willingly behind.

As they hurried through the trees, they stopped every few minutes to see whether they could hear sounds of any pursuers. For about ten minutes they failed to distinguish any. Then, just when Ben was congratulating himself on having thrown the guards off their track, there were shouts behind them. The only consolation was that they seemed a long way off. But Ben knew that among the trees sounds played strange tricks, sometimes the cause of them was nearer than you thought.

'Come on,' he said, urgently, 'We've got to move.'

He knew they were taking a chance by dashing on like this. It meant they were crashing through the trees and making a considerable amount of noise. But he realized on the other hand that they had to keep as great a distance as possible between themselves and their pursuers.

As they ran Ben tried to calculate exactly where they were. Although he had sounded confident when he had told Horace which direction they had to take, his conviction had started to waver about a quarter of an hour ago. Were they going in the right direction, or not? This difficulty was, he had actually only been in these woods once or twice before. He had passed them, of course, when he had ridden from Crossville to Fort Munro. He even knew that they were named Street Woods, after a Mr Street who had once owned them. And who still owned them, as far as he knew.

On impulse he called a halt to their breakneck progress. He held up a hand signaling that he wished to hear if there were any sounds behind them. The rain had stopped. For about half a minute there was nothing. Once again he started to breathe more calmly. Then it happened again. There were the unmistakable shouts of their pursuers. Only this time he was almost positive they were further away than before. In fact they were almost so faint as to be indistinguishable.

'Come on,' he said, urgently.

He could tell from the sun, which he glimpsed every now and again, that they were heading in a southerly direction. This was definitely the right way. They should soon be passing Crossville on their left. That would present some moments of danger. It was possible that somebody or other could be strolling in the woods. It was a very popular venue for courting couples. He himself had brought a young lady here when he had been in his teens. She had just started responding to his passionate kisses when a few young children had chanced upon them. The children had been collecting flowers. Once they saw Ben and his girlfriend they soon made themselves scarce. He had hoped to carry on with the passionate embraces which he'd been enjoying before the interruption by the children. But suddenly his girlfriend's mood had changed. She complained that other children could come across them. So she had suggested he should take her home. It was funny what thoughts occurred when you are running through a wood and hoping against hope that you will not meet anybody.

The hope was short-lived. Suddenly a man was standing in the middle of the path as they rounded a corner. Ben noted that he had several rabbits in a bag. He also had a gun in his hand.

The three stared with surprise stamped on their faces. Horace was the first to react. Before the man could bring up his gun to cover them, Horace had seized the barrel. There was a struggle for supremacy. Ben could do nothing to help Horace, since they were on a narrow path with only room for one person to walk along it.

The struggle was soon over. The man, a slight middle-aged man was no match for Horace. Soon Horace had wrenched the gun from its owner's grasp. Although Ben was standing behind Horace and the path was sheltered by the trees, he could plainly see the fear in the man's eyes. Horace swung the butt of the gun at his head. The man tried to raise his arm to ward off the blow, but he was too late. The butt of the rifle hit his head and with a groan he collapsed on to the ground.

Horace was about to hit the man again, even though he was lying unconscious on the ground, when Ben grabbed his arm.

'That's enough,' he said, sharply.

Horace seemed about to disobey Ben's command, then changed his mind. He shrugged. Next he bent over the man. Ben assumed that he was going to ascertain whether he was still alive. Horace had other ideas. He unhooked the bag containing the dead rabbits from the man's arm.

'We might need these,' he stated.

'Right, let's go,' snapped Ben.

Horace had one other thing on his mind. He searched in the man's pockets.

'For God's sake leave him alone,' hissed Ben.

Horace came up triumphantly with something in his fist. He opened his hand. Ben saw the collection of cartridges he had taken out of the man's pocket.

'You never know when we might need them,' said Horace, showing his teeth in a smile.

CHAPTER 13

Marie stood outside the opera house in Fort Munro. She was impressed how quickly the building had been erected once it had been given the go-ahead. How long was it since it had been started? Six months? And here it was, completed and ready to open at the end of the week.

It would provide her with a new life. Or at least a new start to an old life. She smiled at the thought.

Not that things had been too bad lately. Once Alphonse had recovered from the shock that she was expecting Ben's baby, he had become almost reasonable. Of course much of it had to do with the fact that he needed somebody to take care of him. Somebody to wash his clothes and iron his shirts. Somebody to shine his shoes and trim his hair when it grew too long. Not somebody to share his bed with him – in fact Alphonse had never regarded that activity as of major importance. Anyhow it would have been rather awkward, the way her son was growing in her belly.

Of course at the time she didn't know it was a son. But when he'd been born, six weeks before, the baby turned out to be a boy. She had eagerly searched his face for any resemblance to Ben. The last thing she wanted was that her son should be like that no-good son of a skunk.

To her relief the boy seemed to have many of her features. There was nothing in his face to remind her of Ben. Even Alphonse, when he eventually deigned to look at the baby, announced that the boy looked liked her.

This had pleased her. She had even been more delighted when Alphonse had bought her a present – a large perambulator. He had accompanied the gift with a warning.

'As far as everybody is concerned, that boy

is my son. If you tell anybody otherwise, I'll kick you both out on to the street. Do I make myself clear?'

'Yes, Alphonse,' replied Marie, meekly. 'When would you like your dinner?'

'I've got one or two final arrangements to sort out with the committee, ready for the opening on Saturday. I expect I'll be late.'

At the time he was trying unsuccessfully to tie his bow tie.

'Here, let me,' said Marie.

She tied it expertly. As she watched him walk away from the caravan she reflected once again that fate had been kind to her.

If Ben had reflected about his fate he would definitely have cursed it. As it was, his only concern was to reach his farm safely. They were still following the narrow path through the wood, but he knew that soon they would have to come out into the open. Then there would be about two miles of open country to cross. Two miles which were interspersed with farms. Near the dwellings there would be farm hands working, or maybe the owners of the farms themselves. They would certainly be surprised to see two men, one white and one black, in unmistakable prisoner uniform, running though their fields.

As they ran on Ben tried to work out what they could do when they reached the end of the wood. He considered the possibility of their staying in the wood until nightfall, and then crossing the fields under cover of darkness. That way they could certainly avoid being seen. The trouble was there was a major drawback to the idea. The guards would have informed the sheriff of the escape. The sheriff would have had time to organize a posse. They would have several hours to comb the woods before darkness descended. Not only would they search the woods with the aid of the men in the posse, but also with dogs. And that would spell the end for his and Horace's dash for freedom.

In fact they came to the end of the wood sooner than Ben had anticipated.

'The wood ends here,' said Horace, with surprise.

'I know,' said Ben, surveying the fields in front of them.

'How far is your farm?' demanded Horace.

'About two miles.'

'But, man, they're sure to see us before we get there,' wailed Horace.

There were two men in sight. They were working in a potato field near a farm about a quarter of a mile away. Ben guessed they were hired hands.

'Can't we stay here till night-time,' suggested Horace, hopefully. 'Then we can get to your farm safely.'

'They'll have got a posse together by then. They're bound to catch us,' replied Ben. His gaze was fixed on a row of washing which was fluttering on a line in front of the cottage. The more he gazed at them, the more the idea which had began to germinate, grew. 'What day is it?' he demanded.

'That's a funny question to ask. I can't even tell the time, so how can I be expected to know what day it is?' Horace replied, irritably.

Ben put his hand to the side of his head as he tried to concentrate. Horace watched him with some consternation. Why was his companion concerned about what day it was? Surely they were in enough of a mess without him worrying about unimportant things like that.

'Bells,' said Ben, suddenly. 'That's it!' He hit Horace on the shoulder with excitement.

Horace stared at him in amazement. His large eyes seemed to have grown even larger as he stared at Ben and shook his head with puzzlement.

'I heard the bells yesterday,' exclaimed Ben, still with excitement in his voice.

'If you say so.' Horace shook his head despairingly. The fact that they had escaped as far as this had obviously been too much for Ben. It had affected his mind. Horace was wondering what his next move would be. Whatever it was he would be on his own. He couldn't go on being accompanied by a nutcase like this.

'If I heard bells yesterday, it meant that yesterday was Sunday. In which case today is Monday.' Ben ended on a note of triumph.

'I believe that's the way it is.' Ben would have been the last person he would have expected to go out of his mind. He had always seemed in control of himself.

'So today's market day in Crossville. The chances are there won't be anybody in the farm. They would have gone to market.'

Slowly the point that Ben was making dawned on Horace. The excitement was becoming infectious.

'So the only two around here are those two working in the potato field?'

'Exactly.'

'So if I kill them, then we can go on ahead.' Horace raised his gun.

'Put that down,' said Ben, sharply. 'We won't get far that way.'

Horace reluctantly lowered the gun.

'So what's our next move?' he demanded.

'We wait,' stated Ben.

'But you said that if we wait too long then the posse will catch us.'

'We wait until the men go into the barn to have their chow,' explained Ben. 'It shouldn't be long.'

He was right. It was about ten minutes' later when the two men dug their spades into the soil with the obvious intention of leaving them there until they called back for them. They then headed for the barn which was next to the house. Once inside they were hidden from view. More importantly, they couldn't see Ben and Horace.

Ben waited for a few minutes. Then he said, 'Come on.'

He led the way across the open space. He seemed to be heading for the house. Horace wondered why he had chosen that route. It would have been more sensible to veer to the right and go round the house. That way they would also be going round the back of the barn. Which would mean that if the men came out of the barn unexpectedly, they wouldn't immediately see them. Whereas here they were exposed and if either of the men came out they would see them straight-away.

If Horace was puzzled by Ben's choice of direction he was even more surprised by the fact that he seemed to be heading for the washing-line. Then he suddenly grasped the reason. Of course! If they could steal some clothes then they would stand a better chance of escape. Dressed as they were in convicts' clothes they would be sitting ducks the moment they were spotted by anybody.

'Here!' said Ben, urgently, grabbing trousers and a shirt from the washing-line and thrusting them towards Horace. Ben repeated the action for himself. Then, clutching the clothes under his arm, he raced towards the back of the farm. Horace was only a few yards behind him.

CHAPTER 14

Sylvia Sanderson was listening to the conversation which was going on in the front room. Normally she wasn't an eavesdropper. Indeed as far as she could remember she had never purposely listened to a conversation which she wasn't supposed to overhear. She had been brought up strictly to observe the correct rules of etiquette for a young lady. Her mother had been very insistent on that. She had accepted her mother's guidance and advice without question. Then suddenly her mother had died when she was thirteen years old. She had been distraught. She had sought solace in reading the Bible. For a while she had found some comfort there – particularly in the book of Psalms. But after a while she became less dependent on the Bible. She began to question some of its doctrines, even though she had continued to help her father in many ways with his church work. Then she had met Ben Nolan in jail. His name had never been mentioned in the house since that fateful day. Now, however, a man dressed as some sort of guard had come to the house. His business had obviously been urgent judging by the way he had banged on the front door.

The housemaid had let him in. Sylvia, intrigued by the sudden disturbance, had surreptitiously followed him when he had gone into the study to see her father. Luckily the door was left ajar. Which was why, after six months, she heard the name Ben Nolan mentioned again.

The guard was making no effort to keep his voice down. Sylvia could hear every word clearly.

'Two convicts have escaped from the chain-gang. Ben Nolan is one. The other is a Negro named Horace Thomas. They escaped and ran into Street Wood. We're trying to collect every able person we can to form a posse to comb the wood.'

Sylvia heard her father say: 'I'm afraid I won't be much use to you. I suffer from rheumatism and it's as much as I can do to climb the pulpit steps. I'm sorry.'

'That's all right, reverend,' replied the guard. He hurried out of the front room, obviously intent on going to the next house. He almost bumped into Sylvia, who was trying to get away from her vantage point.

'I'm sorry ma'am,' he apologized.

'You say there are two convicts who have escaped,' she said, ignoring the fact that she shouldn't have listened to the conversation.

'That's right. One of them came from around these parts, I believe. A man of the name of Ben Nolan.'

'Yes, I remember the trial.' Why did she sound so self-possessed when her stomach was churning at the thought of Nolan being hunted down by this guard and his posse?

'I wouldn't worry, ma'am. They're not dangerous. We've got a dozen men combing the woods already. We'll find them before nightfall.' On that confident note he took his leave.

Her father came out of the study.

'Did he tell you about Ben Nolan?' he enquired.

'Yes, Papa,' she replied.

'He was the scoundrel who assaulted you when he was in jail.'

'I know, Papa.'

'I hope they find him and give him a thrashing for trying to escape. I know its an uncharitable thing to say. But no woman is safe when a lecher like that is free, roaming the countryside. Well, I don't suppose we'll hear anything more about him.'

He went back into the study. She went up to her room. If her father only knew. If he ever found out that after the trial she had in fact made it her object to find out where Nolan had lived. It had been comparatively easy. She travelled around the town and the neighbouring farms a great deal as part of her church duties. She used a pony and trap and was a familiar figure as she maybe took food parcels to the needy, or lent a sympathetic ear to a housewife who was in distress, or even provided transport – albeit slow, if a woman wanted her child to go to a school which was too far for walking distance. She had even, on one occasion, acted as a substitute midwife when the real midwife hadn't turned up on time. The experience, although frightening at first had proved exhilarating in the end. And to actually hold the small bundle of humanity in her arms had been one of the happiest moments of her life.

Then one day she came at last to Nolan's farm. It was deserted, of course. She jumped down from the trap by the gate which had been left permanently open. She approached the farm cautiously. She half-expected to see some evidence of life. But there was none. Not even a fieldmouse scuttled across the baked earth in front of the farm. She approached the front door. She knew before she turned the knob that it would be locked. She was right.

As she walked slowly back to the trap she wondered what she had expected to find. Nolan was in a chaingang probably hundreds of miles away. If their paths ever crossed again, which was as unlikely as her becoming an atheist, then he would cut her dead for the part she had played in getting him sentenced. For there was no doubt in her mind that if she hadn't blurted out to her father that Nolan had kissed her in the cell, then the matter would never have arisen in the trial, and the stupid judge would never have used it as further evidence that Nolan should be sentenced to hard labour.

She jumped up into the trap. She turned to give one last searching glance at the farm. It was just as deserted when she had arrived. She didn't know why she was here. Maybe it was idle curiosity. Or was there some deeper reason? A reason which she dared not even start to examine.

CHAPTER 15

The plan had worked. The two convicts no longer looked the part since they had changed into the clothes Ben had stolen from the line. They had changed under the shelter of a hedge. Ben's shirt and trousers had fitted him reasonably well. Horace's on the other hand, were too small.

'It's all right. man,' he informed Ben. 'Us Negros always wear clothes that don't fit us. Nobody will notice any difference.'

Having changed their clothes and then stuffed the convicts' uniforms under the hedge, they were able to set forth without fear of being observed.

'Here,' Horace gave Ben the gun, 'it will look more natural if you've got the gun. If anyone sees us they'll think that I'm your servant. With luck they won't take any notice of us.'

They set out across the fields towards Ben's farm. He knew the terrain like the back of his hand and so was able to avoid the road, where the chances were that somebody would be riding along it. If they did meet somebody on the road, then, since the news hadn't already spread abroad, that rider wouldn't think anything about it. But when the rider reached Crossville and learned that two convicts had escaped, a white man and a black man, the chances were that he would remember meeting them. And the posse would then know which direction to take to catch them.

'How much further, Ben?' demanded Horace, after they had left the wood a mile behind them.

'Not far now,' replied Ben. They were walking quickly, Ben having decided if anyone spotted them they would be less conspicuous if they were walking than running. They had seen several workers in the fields, but they had always been too far away for anyone to identify them. Horace always kept his head turned away from anyone working in the fields so that it wouldn't be apparent that he was black.

They came at last to Stan Wilkins's farm. Ben knew that there was a danger that Stan or one of his farmhands would see him and recognize him. He explained the situation to Horace.

'We'll just have to go the long way round,' he informed him.

'You're the boss,' said Horace, resignedly.

They did take the long way round. It meant their travelling for half an hour instead of ten minutes to reach Ben's farm. However they did eventually reach it. Ben stood by the gate for a few moments to gather his mixed emotions. The last time he had come here it had been to hear about the death of his father. Then he had left the farm as a free man. Here he was returning as a convict. Not only that, but as an escaped convict, which meant that if he were eventually caught, his sentence would automatically be doubled.

114

Horace glanced at him.

'Are you all right, man?'

'Yes, I'm all right. Come on.'

A few minutes later they were inside the house. Ben had forced open the kitchen window with a metal file which he had found in the barn. It was a file he had used in the past to sharpen knives and saws. Now it had served another purpose in giving him leverage to force open the window. He climbed inside and opened the kitchen door for Horace to enter.

Horace glanced around appreciatively.

'Is all this yours, man?' he pointed to the table and chairs, which although dusty, still looked solid and serviceable.

'Yes, it's all mine,' replied Ben, in a choked voice.

'You sit down,' said Horace. 'I'll start a fire and cook some of these rabbits. I could do with a good meal. I don't know the last time I've tasted meat.'

'You start the fire,' said Ben, recovering quickly from his temporary dejection. 'I'll skin the rabbits.'

Half an hour later they were sitting down to a meal of roasted rabbit and potatoes. Ben had managed to dig up some potatoes which had been left growing in the corner of the field.

'Man, that was some meal,' said Horace, appreciatively.

For the first time since entering the house, Ben smiled.

'There's only one thing needed to make it perfect,' said Horace. 'A smoke.'

'I might be able to supply that too,' said Ben.

He climbed the stairs to his bedroom. He went inside and was surprised how little it seemed to have changed. He ran his hands over the sheet on the bed. There was dust there, but not as much as he would have expected. Certainly not as much as below in the kitchen.

The dust was thicker on the dressing-table, though. He ran his finger over it, leaving a line where it had been. He opened the drawer. As he had expected, there was the tin with tobacco inside. The cigarette papers were also there.

He presented them to Horace with a grin.

'Hey! That's just perfect,' smiled Horace, as he carefully rolled a cigarette. There was still enough glow from the embers in the fire to light their smokes. Horace used a spill and then held it for Ben to light his. They both took a long pull.

'Who'd have thought we'd be living like this a few hours ago?' demanded Horace, with a contented smile.

Their moment of bliss was short-lived. They both heard it at the same time. It was the unmistakable sound of approaching horsemen.

'The posse is here already,' cried Horace.

CHAPTER 16

Sylvia walked agitatedly up and down her bedroom. Why was she so concerned about what would happen to Nolan? She had only met him once, in jail. The other time, when she had seen him in court, she didn't count.

Why had he made such an impression on her? They had only talked together briefly for a few minutes. Then he had kissed her. Without her consent. So she'd slapped his face. It had been what he had richly deserved. So why was she so concerned about him.

Was it because he had kissed her? She had been kissed by several young men before. There was nothing new in being kissed. Come on, who are you trying to deceive? It was the way he had kissed her that had stayed in her mind. It kept coming back to her, unbidden, at odd moments. Often when she was about to go to sleep. It was the way he had kissed her as if he intended the kiss to go on and on and on. It had brought moments of undiluted pleasure which she had never known before.

She even had fantasies about being kissed by him again. Of course, not in jail. But maybe in some leafy wood. Or on a hillside when the wild flowers were in bloom. She had been in the cell long enough to realize that he was a handsome man. A very handsome man. The sort of man that a girl would be pleased to walk out with.

And now he was an escaped convict. She knew that it was only a matter of time before they found him. It was obvious that he would head for his farm. Probably the hunt for him and his companion was being led by guards like the one who had come to the house ten minutes before. This could possibly give him an hour or so start since the guards wouldn't know the whereabouts of his farm. But once the guards approached the sheriff with their problem, then the sheriff would be able to tell them where Nolan lived. After that it wouldn't be long before the posse caught up with him and his companion.

She came to a sudden decision. She ran downstairs to her father's study. He looked up, surprised, at her sudden entrance.

'I'm taking the pony and trap,' she announced. 'There are some visits I must make.'

'Do you think it's wise?' said her father. 'There are a couple of escaped convicts not too far away according to the guard who just called here. One of them is Ben Nolan, the man who assaulted you in jail.'

'The guard said they had gone through Street Wood. I'll be going in the opposite direction. Anyhow, they've probably been recaptured by now.'

'Yes, well if you're going the other side of town, you should be safe enough. Who are you going to visit?'

'Mrs Crowe. She lives far enough away

from Street Wood.'

In normal circumstances she would never dream of lying to her father. But these weren't normal circumstances, she told herself, as she kissed him lightly on the cheek.

She hurried into the kitchen. What would a convict on the loose need? Food, obviously. Luckily she had half a loaf of bread and some cheese on hand, which in fact she had intended taking to one of the more destitute parishioners. She hastily shoved them in her basket. She added some apples and a piece of ham which she had intended serving up for their supper. As an afterthought she dashed upstairs to her bedroom. She dived into her dressing-room table and grabbed a bundle of notes. She had intended banking them but they could possibly provide Nolan with a means of escape. Maybe he could get to Fort Munro. It was only thirteen miles away. Once there he could catch the train and then he would be safe.

She dashed downstairs and out through

the back door.

'She seems in an awful hurry to go to visit Mrs Crowe,' said the minister thoughtfully. He listened to the sound of the pony's hoofs as Sylvia urged the animal out of the yard and on to the road.

CHAPTER 17

Ben and Horace counted the riders as they approached the gate leading to the farm. There were six of them. They had rushed up to their vantage point in the front bedroom when they heard the sound of the horses' hoofs.

'Shall I start shooting?' demanded Horace. He had grabbed the gun from its position propped up in the kitchen before he had dashed up the stairs following Ben.

'No,' Ben said sharply. 'There are six of them and only two of us. Besides we've only got one gun between us.'

The leader had now swung through the gate into the yard in front of the house.

'I'm not going to die without a fight,' said Horace, grimly. He held his gun at the ready, pointing to the leader.

'There's something odd about them,' announced Ben. 'I don't think they're the posse.'

'What do you mean?' demanded Horace, staring intently at them.

'I can't see a guard among them,' said Ben. 'They look like riders who have come a long way, not just a few miles from the railway line.'

It was true. There wasn't a guard among them. In fact they looked more like a bunch of outlaws than the ordinary citizens the guards would have gathered together to form a posse.

'And there's only six of them,' said Horace, eagerly. 'If it's a posse it would be bigger.'

'Exactly,' said Ben. 'The question is, who are they?'

By now they had all entered the yard in front of the farm. They began to dismount.

'Maybe they just want to water their horses,' said Horace.

The horses were steaming and showed

every sign of having been ridden hard for a considerable time.

'Let's hope that's all they want,' said Ben. 'We'll just have to keep quiet and hope they'll go away.'

'The first one that comes up the stairs will get a bellyful of lead,' said Horace, threateningly.

'Just keep your head down,' said Ben.

They could soon hear the newcomers moving around downstairs. At first Ben had harboured hopes that they might help themselves to water and then leave. But when he considered the situation more carefully he realized there was a flaw in his assumption. Once those below went into the kitchen they would see the evidence that two people had recently had a meal there. They would see the rabbit bones on the plates and the coffee cups. It would be immediately obvious that the two people had had a meal fairly recently judging by the warm coffee left in the cups.

All of which meant that the two of them

were in a precarious position. The only slight ray of hope was the fact that the unexpected visitors were obviously not the posse. This was confirmed when a few minutes later a voice shouted up the stairs.

'Hey! You two up there, come on down.'

Ben knew it was useless trying to deny their whereabouts. The new arrivals had obviously reached the barn and the dairy. Since there was no sign of two people in either of them it left only one other possibility. That the two who had been drinking their coffee when they had been interrupted, were hiding upstairs.

'Come on, Goldilocks,' shouted the voice. 'Or Daddy Bear will begin to get annoyed.'

There was general laughter from the others.

Ben moved to the bedroom door. He signalled Horace to give him the rifle. Horace hesitated, then reluctantly handed it over.

'If Daddy Bear comes up the stairs, he'll get his head blown off,' said Ben.

He opened the bedroom door quickly,

fired a shot down the stairs and closed the door while before the sound of the shot had died away.

There was a pause. Then, 'Daddy Bear doesn't like guns,' said the voice. 'Nor being shot at. If you don't come down with your hands in the air by the time I count up to three, then Daddy Bear will take some of the nice fire you left in the grate and set fire to the farm. Do I make myself clear?'

A chill ran through Ben at the thought of having his home destroyed by fire. He did not doubt for a moment that the stranger would keep his threat. Although pretending to play a children's game, the threat was somehow even more sinister.

'Who are you?' demanded Ben.

'Well, we're not the law,' said the voice. There was a burst of laughter from his companions.

'Why don't you just take what you want and go,' said Ben.

'You don't understand. We've come a long way. We want to rest up for a few days. How can we sleep in peace knowing that you're up there with guns?'

'Tell them we're escaped convicts,' said Horace, urgently.

Ben hesitated. It had sounded as though his original guess had been right and the gang downstairs were indeed outlaws. If so they were brothers under the skin, since he and Horace were both definitely not on the side of the law.

'We're escaped convicts,' Ben announced. 'So you see we're not on the side of the law, either.'

There was silence while the voice digested the information. Then the voice replied: 'Come on down. Maybe we can do a deal.'

Ben glanced at Horace.

'If we join up with some outlaws,' said Horace, 'maybe there'll be safety in numbers.'

Yes, maybe, thought Ben. Also there was one other consideration. The outlaws, if that's what they were, had been pulling two spare horses behind them. If he and Horace were to get away from this place they would need horses. So maybe the horses would come in useful.

'We're coming down,' said Ben.

'Throw your gun down first,' said the voice.

Ben knew that he had no choice but to comply. He opened the bedroom door and regretfully tossed the gun down the stairs.

'Right. Now you two come down and meet Daddy Bear,' said the voice.

CHAPTER 18

Sylvia drove as quickly as the old pony would trot. She fretted at the time it was taking them to reach Nolan's farm. The only consolation was the fact that so far she had seen no sign of a posse. She guessed she was at least half an hour or so in front of them. God willing she would be able to meet Nolan, give him the provisions she had brought, and watch him escape to safety.

There were no doubts in her mind that she was acting on the best of Christian instincts. She was helping a human being in distress as the good Samaritan had helped the Jew. True, Nolan was an escaped convict but, during the past few months, whenever she had thought about him, which had been often, she had never regarded him as a convict. She thought of him as a man who had been wronged. Of a man more sinned against than sinning.

In the first place he had killed the other man in a fair fight. There had been no suggestion that Nolan had drawn first. So if he had killed the other in a fair fight why had he been convicted? Largely because the judge, Judge Pearson, was a hypocrite.

He was strongly against anyone carrying firearms, which was perfectly reasonable. But she knew for a fact that his son, Henry, had been convicted of shooting a man and had been tried in Fort Munro. The gossip was – and she was good at collecting gossip since she travelled round the town listening to much of it daily – that Judge Pearson had used his influence to get his son released. Henry, whom she remembered in school as being a particularly obnoxious youth, had walked away scot free. Yet, here was Nolan being punished for the same crime.

His farm finally came into sight. She was about a quarter of a mile away from it but her heart lifted when she spied it in the distance. Her joy, however, was short-lived. The posse had arrived there before her! There were several horses tethered to the fence at the front of the house.

For a moment she couldn't believe her eyes. How could the posse have arrived there before her? It must have taken a short cut across the fields. Yet less than half an hour ago the guard had been trying to form a posse. She shook her head in puzzlement.

Well, whatever reservations she had about the speed of the posse's arrival, there was no doubt that they were there. She had instinctively reined in the pony when she had seen the horses. She now sat disconsolate, staring at the farm ahead. So far there had been no sign of the posse who she assumed were inside the farm.

Common sense told her that she should turn back. She had arrived too late. She had lost the race to save Nolan. The guards would take him back to the chaingang. She would probably never see him again.

Her heart felt heavy at the thought. It was

suddenly as if she had grown a year older in the space of a few minutes. She knew she would now have to put him out of her mind for ever. She would have to banish the picture of his handsome face, with fair wavy hair and light blue eyes, for ever. She knew that she had a source of comfort in prayer, but it would take regular daily prayers to help her finally forget him.

Suddenly she was aware of a rider racing towards her. Or rather racing along the road in her direction. He was obviously on his way back to Crossville. He must be a guard or one of the posse. As he came nearer she saw that he wasn't a guard and he was rather too shabbily dressed to be a member of the posse. Suddenly, for some unaccountable reason, fear clutched at her heart. She had an overwhelming desire to turn round and go as fast as the pony would take her back towards Crossville.

There couldn't be any grounds for such an unwarranted panic could there? He was now near enough for her to see the expression on his face. It was a face full of hatred and it was staring straight at her. This time she didn't hesitate. She jerked on the reins savagely and forced the pony round in a tight circle. She knew even as she did so that she was too late. In a few moments the reins were snatched from her.

The rider put his face close to hers so that she could smell his foul breath.

'You're coming with me,' he snarled. 'We don't like spies. And we know exactly how to deal with them.'

CHAPTER 19

In Fort Munro Alphonse was in the opera house, surveying the last-minute alterations. One of the gas chandeliers wasn't working. The curtains weren't coming fully together as they should do. The star of the show, a conjurer named Dino, had sent a telegram that he was ill and wouldn't be able to turn up. Where would he find a replacement? He only had half the orchestra he should have. And there were other gaps in acts. The show was due to start in five days' time and everything was chaotic.

It was all that committee's fault. If they hadn't insisted on a mixed bill to try to satisfy everybody then he could have gone ahead with his original plan and put on an opera. But now it was too late. He stared at the billboard announcing the various acts though he already knew it by heart.

The show would be opened by Charles Lawson doing his famous Shakespearian monologues. He couldn't stand the man. The fact that he drank too much didn't help. He would have liked to put him further down the list but he had been forced to bring Lawson on first in the hope that he wouldn't have had time to get drunk. He knew he would have to watch him closely while he was on stage. At the first indication of a slurred word or phrase he would cut his act short and bring him off. The last thing he wanted was for the audience to be laughing their heads off in the middle of Hamlet's soliloquy.

Then there were Treena and Tom, the dwarfs. He had been forced to give them a spot on the bill to help to fill it. He knew they were dependable and didn't drink. They would perform their tumbling routines as they had done dozens of times for him when he had been running the circus in the tent. They would be guaranteed to get a lot of applause.

They would be followed by Kitty, the Irish Thrush. She would bring the house down with her sweet voice and choice of melodies. In the second part of the show, after the interval, when she went into her routine singing the Civil War songs and dressing up first in a Confederate uniform and then as a Republican it was a guaranteed finale which would send everyone away happy.

The rest of the bill was filled up with dancers, impressionists and comedians – none of which was particularly memorable. Still, nobody could expect miracles – in fact he had done well to get them all together in such a short space of time. There was one thing he had been lucky with – he had found a knife-thrower to replace Nolan. The guy's name was Ed Treadle. He wasn't as good as Nolan – the distances between Marie and the knives were far more than when Nolan had been throwing them. But beggars can't be choosers. Anyhow it made a good finish for the first act.

Thinking of Nolan made his blood boil. In the beginning he had assumed that Marie was as responsible as Nolan for their affair. But lately Marie had been so docile and willing to grant his every wish that he now couldn't bring himself to imagine that she had been a willing party to the seduction. No, it was definitely Nolan who had been at fault. He should never have hired him in the first place. In the first place he was too handsome. And in the second place he had the sort of smile which would twist women round his little finger.

At the moment, however Ben was far from smiling. He was staring at the apparition which Quincey had brought in. It was a kicking, struggling, dishevelled Sylvia. The outlaw flung her down in the middle of the floor like a sack of potatoes.

Ben involuntarily moved forward to help to pick her up. The *click* of a revolver warned him against being too impetuous. Ben knew that it was the leader of the gang, Tooley, who had cocked the gun. Nevertheless he ignored him and picked her up. Her eyes found his and a flash of recognition passed between them. Ben followed it with a quick shake of his head as he helped her to her feet.

'Here, give the lady your chair.'

The remark was directed by Tooley at another member of the gang, Wilton. It was punctuated by a kick which caught Wilton in the kidneys. The recipient of the blow groaned. The rest of the gang laughed.

Seated on the kitchen chair, Sylvia was forced to face Tooley who stood, legs apart, in front of her.

'Now, you'd better start talking, young lady,' he said, not unkindly.

'Who are you? And why have you brought me here?' she demanded with an outward show of bravery, although inwardly her stomach was churning.

'If you tell us who you are, we'll tell you who we are.' This time there was a threatening note in Tooley's voice.

Sylvia held her head high. 'My name is Sylvia Sanderson. I'm the minister's daughter.'

'She's the minister's daughter,' said another member of the gang, Minkley, in an effeminate voice.

The others laughed.

'I'm beginning to get impatient,' snapped Tooley. 'You've only answered half my question.'

'I'm taking provisions for one of the poorer ladies of the parish. She's a widow. Her name is Mrs Crowe.'

'That's right, boss,' said the outlaw who had brought her in, a man named Williams. 'She's got some victuals in her saddle-bag.'

At the mention of victuals there was a general hubbub among the outlaws.

'All right, you scum go outside and share it out between you,' said Tooley. 'I've got some more questions to ask. And I still want to know more about you two,' he swung round so that his revolver was now covering Ben and Horace who, having been forced to join the outlaws, had been standing in the corner, waiting for Tooley to make a further move.

CHAPTER 20

'Right, I think it's your turn to answer a few more questions,' Tooley had turned to Ben.

'What do you want to know?' demanded Ben.

'A few minutes ago when you picked the young lady up from the floor I spotted a look of recognition between the two of you. How did that come about?'

Ben answered quickly to prevent Sylvia blurting out the wrong answer.

'I was tried in Crossville six months ago. She must have seen me at the trial.'

'Why were you tried?'

'I shot a man in a saloon.'

'So you're a killer?' Tooley stared at Ben, thoughtfully. 'So that's why they put you in jail?'

'They put us in a chaingang,' said Horace,

hotly. 'Here, I'll show you.' He pulled up his trousers revealing the mark where the chain had bitten into his leg.

'All right, I'll come to you later.' Tooley waved a dismissive hand towards Horace. 'So you're good with a gun.' He had turned his attention back to Ben.

'Fairly good.'

'Let's see how good.' Tooley emptied the bullets from one of his revolvers. He tossed the gun to Ben. Then he took off his belt and handed it over.

Ben strapped on the belt. He put the revolver in holster. He tried a few slow draws while Tooley looked on.

'All right,' said Tooley. 'I'll count up to three. When I reach three, you draw.'

Ben nodded. Tooley started to count. When he reached three there was a sudden blur of movement, then the gun in Ben's hand was pointing at Tooley's heart.

'That was quick. Very quick,' said Tooley, appreciatively. 'But this is the first and last time you will ever point a gun at me. Do you

143

understand?' He underlined the threat by raising his own gun and pointing it at Ben's chest.

'You're the boss,' said Ben, drily.

'Make sure you remember that,' said Tooley. 'Now the problem is, what are we going to do with you, young lady?' He turned his attention to Sylvia.

She shivered as she stared into his cold, calculating eyes. She tried to meet his stare, but failed. She dropped her eyes and found herself staring at the floor.

'I think in fact you will come in useful. Very useful.'

One of the outlaws came in.

'It's all right,' said Tooley. 'We were just discussing what to do with the evangelist.'

The outlaw glanced at Sylvia. He licked his lips appreciatively.

'Me and the boys have been missing female company for the past few weeks. If you give her to us, maybe we could do a bit of catching up.'

Sylvia's pale complexion turned even

lighter as she realized the full implications of the outlaw's words.

'I don't see why not,' said Tooley, thoughtfully. 'But I don't want her to become too damaged … I've got other plans for her afterwards.'

Sylvia had closed her eyes. This couldn't be happening to her. Not to a minister's daughter. What they were calmly proposing was the fate worse than death. Or who knew? When they had finished with her, perhaps death itself would be her next step. She opened her eyes and stared appealingly at Ben. Why didn't he say something? After all she come here because of him. He was the reason why she was in this terrible position. No, that wasn't fair. Even in her distress she could still think clearly. He hadn't invited her here. She had arrived entirely by her own volition.

Ben finally spoke up. 'I don't think you'll have time for your men to enjoy themselves.'

Enjoy themselves? How could he use such words? There couldn't be any pleasure in what Tooley was contemplating, letting his men loose with her as the victim.

Tooley stared thoughtfully at Ben. 'Why not?'

'We told you we're convicts on the run. We're only about half an hour at the most in front of the posse. When they realize that we've come here, they'll surround the house. Then it won't only be goodbye to us, but it will be goodbye to you too.' Ben spoke matter-of-factly as though he was just outlining a mundane daily event.

'If, as you say, the posse is only about half an hour behind you, how will they know where you are? They'll probably track you down eventually, but you could have gone anywhere. You could have taken any direction out of Crossville.'

'They'll know where I am, because this is my house,' said Ben, flatly.

'Well, well, fancy that,' drawled Tooley. 'No wonder you came down like a scalded cat when I said I was going to set fire to the place.'

146

The outlaw who was standing by the door spoke up.

'Does that mean we're going to have wait until later before we have our fun?'

'I'm afraid so, Glen. But maybe you won't have to wait too long.'

Ben was staring at the outlaw. Glen. Glen Hillier. Of course! He remembered the drawing of his father's killer. It bore a faint resemblance to the outlaw. Anyhow, all he had to do was to confirm that that his surname was Hillier. This should be fairly easy since they were obviously going to travel with the outlaws. It seemed that Tooley had plans for him, otherwise he wouldn't have asked him to draw to see how quickly he could do so.

Tooley was staring at him thoughtfully. Ben would have to be careful, the gang leader was obviously no fool.

'Something on your mind, Nolan?' demanded Tooley.

'No, I was just wondering which way you were heading? If the posse is coming from the direction of Crossville it would be safer to take the road to Fort Munro.'

'I've already worked that out,' said Tooley, drily. He turned to the outlaw by the door. 'Tell the others to get ready. We're moving in five minutes.'

CHAPTER 21

In the Pinkerton office in Chicago, Burke was sitting behind his desk, as usual. Grey, however, was standing in front of the desk, which was rather unusual, since usually Burke invited him to sit down. But not this afternoon.

'I've had a telegram.' Burke tapped the yellow paper which he was holding in his hand.

'Who from?' demanded Grey. He was annoyed that Burke hadn't invited him to sit down.

'That doesn't concern you,' said Burke, sharply. 'It's what's in the telegram that's important.'

So important as to keep me standing here instead of letting me sit down? thought Grey. Aloud he said, 'Is it from one of our agents?'

'It's from one of our spies,' said Burke, heavily.

'I see.' It had always been a matter of disagreement between the two men that Burke controlled the couple of dozen or so men who were called spies. Burke never divulged the names of any of them to Grey. It seemed to Grey that Burke, in not confiding in him the identities of these men, was saying in effect that he didn't trust him.

'This one is a member of a well-known gang of outlaws.' Burke tapped the telegram with his forefinger.

'I see,' said Grey, even more coldly than before.

'The gang are planning to rob an opera house.'

'An opera house?' This time Grey's voice registered surprise.

'In...' Burke consulted the telegram. 'Fort Munro.'

'But why should they want to rob an opera house? What are they going to steal. The band's instruments?'

'That's what you'll have to find out.' There was satisfaction in Burke's voice. He was sending the self-righteous prig away for a few days. It would be nice not to see his face around the office for at least a week.

'But what can I do?' There was a hint of panic in his voice.

'Go to Fort Munro!' Burke added, 'That's an order.'

'I can understand a gang robbing a train, or a bank, but not an opera house.' Grey grasped at the straw that perhaps Burke's spy had made a mistake. Maybe there wouldn't be a robbery after all.

'It says here,' Burke consulted the telegram again, 'that there will be a grand opening on Saturday. You know what that means?'

'It means that the rich people in Fort Munro will be there,' said Grey, unable to keep the disappointment out of his voice.

'Exactly,' said Burke, triumphantly. 'It means that the wives will be wearing their pearls and diamonds. The men will have pocketbooks full of dollar bills. The outlaws will probably have more pickings than if they had robbed a bank.'

Grey accepted that there was no way out. The only thing he could do would be to go to Fort Munro and keep his head down when the robbery started.

'What about the sheriff?' he demanded.

'I've already sent him a telegram,' stated Burke. 'I told him that you will call to see him when you arrive in Fort Munro.'

'I'll want a gunman,' stated Grey.

'You can take Evans. It's a pity that Nolan is in jail. He would be ideal as a back-up man.'

In fact Ben was riding like the wind in the direction of Fort Munro. Sylvia was on the horse, too, clinging to him.

Ben had argued with Tooley that there was no need to take Sylvia with them. That if they just left her there she couldn't possibly harm the gang, since she didn't know where they were heading for. Tooley's reply had been that she knew who the members of the gang were. If necessary she could identify them.

In fact, although she was fully aware of the precariousness of her position, Sylvia felt strangely happy. She was close to Ben. In fact she couldn't be closer, she reflected, as she held on with her arms around him. True, when they came to Fort Munro, circumstances would change. She would be tossed back into the cauldron of argument about what was going to happen to her. For the moment, however, she could even view it dispassionately. Whatever happened in the future, she was confident that Ben would defend her. Tooley had obviously been impressed with the speed with which Ben had drawn his gun. Whatever Tooley had in mind when they reached Fort Munro then Ben was obviously destined to play a part in Tooley's plan. Therefore Ben would be in a strong position in the gang. So if it came to a showdown, Ben would be able to defend her. She clung even closer to him, seeking further reassurance in their closeness. She wondered if Ben was thinking about her.

Ben in fact was thinking about a certain outlaw – one by the name of Glen. The more he thought about him the more he was convinced that, in fact, he was Glen Hillier. He had studied his face in the few minutes when the gang were getting ready to move on. Of course the outlaw, like all the others, had several weeks' growth of beard. This made a positive identification tricky. But from what he could remember of the drawing in the sheriff's office the man who was now riding ahead of him certainly resembled Hillier. Of course all he had to do was to wait until they reached their destination. There, if he bided his time, he would definitely be able to find out the outlaw's surname.

He was conscious of the girl behind clinging fiercely to him. What had she got herself into? Or rather what sort of hand had fate dealt to get her involved like this? It seemed that she had been in the wrong place at the wrong time. If she hadn't been riding along the road in her pony and trap she wouldn't now be in the precarious position in which she found herself. True, she was safe for the time being. But who could say what would happen to her once they had reached Fort Munro? Maybe Tooley would toss her to the none too tender mercies of the gang of outlaws. From their appearance and remarks it would be safe to assume that they had been deprived of female company for some time. For a long while in fact. And the person behind him was every inch a female – a fact he was conscious of as she pressed closely against him.

CHAPTER 22

In Crossville the Reverend Sanderson was going frantic. News had just reached him that his daughter's pony and trap had been discovered outside the farmhouse where the criminal, Nolan, had lived. A couple of hours ago, when the guard had arrived at his house telling him that Nolan and a black man had escaped from the chaingang and he was trying to form a posse, he had thought little of it. Even when Sylvia had taken the pony and trap a few minutes later and driven off in unseemly haste, he had thought little of it. Even when she had failed to return for a couple of hours he hadn't become too worried. Sylvia often rode off for hours on end, delivering small parcels of food to the deserving poor. He differentiated between the deserving poor and the undeserving, of course, since there were one or two families who had moved into the locality who seemed to have no intention of working hard for a living. They seemed to be just content on accepting charity. He had always told Sylvia to beware of such spongers.

This time she had said she was going to visit Mrs Crowe. She was a widow whose cottage was about two miles outside Crossville. It was due west of the town. But Sylvia's pony and trap had been found to the east of the town. That was where Nolan had lived.

Coupled with the worry about Sylvia's whereabouts was the disturbing thought that his daughter had deceived him. It was more than likely that she had had no intention of visiting Mrs Crowe. It was now a possibility – no, a distinct probability, that she had intended visiting the criminal, Nolan, once she had heard the news of his escape. No doubt she had found out where he had lived while she was on her charitable rounds. She had even intended for Nolan the food she had taken under the guise of taking it for Mrs Crowe.

There was a knock at the door. He hurried to answer it before the maid could emerge from the kitchen. It was a guard, not the one who had originally called at the house. This one was older, white-haired, in his forties.

'Have you any news?' There was a tremor in his voice.

'I'm afraid not. We've searched the area around Nolan's farm.'

'There was no sign of her? That could mean – anything?'

'Exactly. There was one puzzling feature though.'

'What was that?'

'There were recent prints of several horses' hoofs. In fact our Indian scout counted eight horses.'

'Eight horses? What do you think that means?'

'It probably meant that eight horsemen arrived at the farm either before or after your daughter.'

'That's the only clue there is?' He couldn't keep the disappointment out of his voice.

'Well, there is one other slight piece of evidence which might help us. Apparently the riders – they're more likely to be outlaws – ate some food outside the farm. Our scout found some small bones which were probably rabbit bones. Would you know whether your daughter took any food with her in the pony and trap.'

'She was always taking victuals round for the poor. She made a trip on most days.'

'And today?'

'She did say she was going out. She said she was taking a food parcel to Mrs Crowe. She's a poor widow.'

'And where does Mrs Crowe live?'

The minister hesitated before replying. Eventually he said, 'She lives due west of the town. About two miles along the road.'

'I see.' The guard emphasized the words. 'And Nolan's farm is to the east of the town?'

The minister didn't bother to reply. A

couple of minutes ago he had been thinking of asking the guard into the house, but now he was glad that he hadn't since, from his expression, he had obviously guessed that Sylvia had deceived him.

The guard's next question irritated him even further.

'Do you know whether your daughter ever contacted the prisoner while he has been serving his sentence?'

'Of course she hasn't.' He was aware that he was protesting vehemently. Possibly too vehemently.

'It seems strange that she would visit his farm not long after he had escaped from the chain-gang.' The guard pursued the matter.

'She believed in charity,' the minister snapped.

'I see,' said the guard, heavily. It again wasn't exactly obvious what he did see.

'Shouldn't you be going about your duty trying to find my daughter?' asked the minister, icily.

'There is one further piece of information,'

the guard replied, as he turned to leave. 'The outlaws – I think we can safely assume that they are outlaws – were heading for Fort Munro when they left Nolan's farm.'

'Do you think they took Sylvia with them?' demanded her father.

'I don't know. It seems likely, though.'

CHAPTER 23

The outlaws had arrived on a mountain overlooking Fort Munro later than they had expected. One of the horses had lost a shoe and so the whole party had been forced to travel at a walking pace for the last six miles or so. They dismounted at the spot chosen by Tooley. It was a couple of miles above the town with a convenient stream nearby.

'Right,' said Tooley to Sylvia. 'You can make yourself useful. There are some tins of beans in that saddle-bag. When we've got a fire going you can cook them for us. You can cook, I suppose?' he added, sarcastically.

'Of course I can,' she snapped.

Tooley grinned. 'All right. You can show us.' He turned to the men who were taking their saddles off their horses. 'Nobody touches her, do you understand? If they do,

I'll shoot their ears off. I've got plans for her.'

There were mutterings of discontent from a couple of the outlaws.

'You promised we could have her,' said the outlaw called Glen.

'Yes, well you'll have to wait until later, Hillier,' snapped Tooley.

He was right. Ben could hardly conceal his satisfaction. It was Hillier, even under that growth of beard. Fate had delivered him to within a few yards of him. All he had to do was to bide his time. Then, when the opportunity arose, he would kill him. Exactly as he had promised his dead father.

'Will you open the beans for me?' Sylvia's voice interrupted his thoughts.

'Right.'

Sylvia had emptied the saddle-bag of the tins of beans. Ben approached Tooley.

'Could you let me have a knife?'

Tooley, who was talking to one of the outlaws, handed Ben his knife without turning round. As Sylvia handed each tin to

Ben, he opened them with the knife. Sylvia smiled her thanks but Ben's thoughts were elsewhere.

At present he didn't have an instrument to kill Hillier. He obviously didn't have a gun. The alternative would be a knife. Like the one he held in his hand, which Tooley had produced from his belt. It was shorter than the ones he used to handle when he threw them at Marie. That now seemed like years ago. But even with this knife he knew he could inflict enough damage to kill Hillier. He held it thoughtfully in his hand, having opened the last tin for Sylvia.

Tooley turned and spotted him.

'If you're waiting for any more tins, that's all we've got until tomorrow.'

'Right,' said Ben.

His hopes of keeping the knife were shattered by Tooley's next remark. 'And I'll have my knife back.' He held out his hand.

By the time they had finished supper it was growing dark. The blankets were unloaded from the horses and Tooley tossed one to Ben.

'Here, you'll have to share with the evangelist. Don't forget what I said about damaged goods.'

Ben arranged the blanket on the ground, at a slight distance away from the fire.

'Which side of the bed do you sleep on?' he asked Sylvia.

It took her a moment to realize that it was a joke. How could he joke at a moment like this? She had never slept close to a man in her life. Yet here she would be sleeping near a man who was virtually a stranger. The fact that she liked him had nothing to do with it. She knew nothing about him. What if he touched her during the night? After all, he had already kissed her once without her permission. Who could she appeal to for help? Not any of the other outlaws, who were all arranging themselves as near the fire as they could.

Sylvia did what she always did before going to bed. She put her hands together and prayed. Ben waited patiently until she had finished.

'Is this all right?' He was lying on his side so that his back was towards her.

'I suppose so,' she said, icily.

She turned so that her back was towards him. She deliberately left a gap of a couple of feet between them.

She thought of her own cosy bed. Usually she had two blankets over her. Here there was only one between them. Her own bed was comfortable, not like this hard piece of mountainside. In her own bed she always had a pillow. Here there was nothing. She usually read for a short while before turning out the lamp. Here the only source of light was a cold moon. In her own bedroom her father always came up to see her and say good-night, before kissing her. Here there was nobody, except the stranger who was lying next to her.

Suddenly, without warning, she burst into tears. For a few moments there was no reaction from Ben. Then he turned.

'It's all right,' he said, taking her in his

arms. 'Everything will be all right, I promise.'

She cried herself to sleep, not knowing that for ages afterwards Ben held her in his arms. At last he kissed her lightly on the forehead and placed her carefully on the blanket.

CHAPTER 24

Tooley's announcement the following morning took them all by surprise.

'Right, you've all been wondering what our next job will be.'

'A bank?' suggested one.

'A railway?' ventured another.

'No. We're going to the opera.'

He roared with laughter at the surprise on their faces.

'So he's actually built an opera house,' said Ben, wonderingly.

'What do you know about it?' demanded Tooley.

'It's Alphonse, isn't it? He always said that one day he'd build an opera house. And now he's done it.'

'So what do you know about him?' persisted Tooley.

'I used to work for him,' confessed Ben. 'I worked for him for a couple of years. In those days he ran an open-air circus.'

'When you say you worked for him, what exactly did you do?' demanded one of the outlaws.

Ben decided not to reveal that he was a knife-thrower.

'I was a sharpshooter,' he announced.

'He's good. I can vouch for that,' stated Tooley.

'He's just what we need – a man who's good with a gun,' said another outlaw.

'I'll have a talk with you later.' Tooley addressed the remark to Ben. 'In the meantime you're all going to town to get smartened up.'

'My girlfriend thinks I'm smart enough as I am,' said the scruffiest of the outlaws. The others laughed.

'When do we start?' said another.

'Not we – you,' said Tooley. Puzzlement was stamped on the faces of the outlaws. 'If we all ride down to Fort Munro we'll be spotted as outlaws before we reach the main street. For one thing there are eight of us. And for another thing we've been on the run for the last few weeks – we haven't had a bath or a shave or a haircut.'

'So if we don't all go down together, what do we do?'

'We go down in pairs. That way we won't be conspicuous. Hillier and Morgan will go down first.'

'If we're going to have a haircut, shave and bath, it'll cost money,' stated Hillier.

'I know that,' said Tooley. 'You'll each have ten dollars. That'll pay for you to pretty yourselves up and have a steak meal. I'll want you back here in about three hours. That'll give two more a chance to go down this afternoon and do the same thing. Any questions?'

'I suppose the robbery is set for Saturday,' stated Morgan.

'That's right,' said Tooley.

'That's three days' time. In that time my beard will have grown again.'

'That won't matter,' said Tooley. 'You'll be as smart as many of the cowboys who'll be coming to the opera.'

The two saddled up to raucous comments from some of the others.

'Don't spend all your money in the brothel,' said one.

'There'll be plenty of chance for that after the robbery,' said Tooley, sternly.

Sylvia had moved further away to dissociate herself from the comments of the outlaws. Ben hesitated, then followed her.

'Don't take too much notice of them,' he advised.

'They're scum,' she said, coldly.

'Where's your Christian charity?' he asked.

'I left it behind when they kidnapped me,' she snapped.

She really was bristly this morning. Well, it was not surprising, a girl like her with her upbringing, being forced to listen to the lewd comments of the cowboys.

'I believe I made a fool of myself last night,' she announced.

'How do you mean?'

'I was crying, wasn't I? I'm sorry. It won't happen again.'

Tooley came over.

'I want to know about this guy, Alphonse. What kind of person is he?'

Ben described the circus and the people working in it. Sylvia sat cross-legged on the ground and listened, fascinated. The only fictional part was that he described himself as part of a sharpshooting duo instead of his knife-throwing act.

'Why did you leave the circus?' asked Sylvia.

Ben knew that now was his chance. He had guessed that yesterday Sylvia had really been calling at his farm with the provisions she had brought. Her story about calling round at neighbouring farms didn't hold water. There weren't any neighbouring farms except Stan Wilkins's and he would hardly have been accepting gifts of food from the church. No, Sylvia had learned about their escape from the chaingang. She had assumed that he would be heading for his farm, and that was how she had arrived there so quickly. The only question was why had she done it? The obvious answer was that she felt sorry for him because she had been partly instrumental in getting him sentenced in the first place. If she had kept quiet about the kiss in jail then probably his sentence would have been reduced. Unfortunately there was one other complication. He had noticed the way she had occasionally looked at him He had had enough experience with women to recognize the look as one in which the woman was wondering how far their relationship could develop. Well in Sylvia's case, the answer was no further. He had sworn to avenge his father's murder and a woman would definitely be in the way. Even a woman as attractive as the one who was now staring at him intently waiting for his answer.

'I got Alphonse's wife pregnant,' he stated, calmly.

CHAPTER 25

The audience were filing into the opera house. There were gasps of surprised delight at seeing the décor. Most of the men and women stopped just inside the entrance to admire the number of chandeliers. Then there was the curtain which concealed the stage with its beautiful red-and-gold woven pattern. The curved balcony was a sight to behold – Alphonse had managed to include among his workforce some wood-turners who had produced the exquisite carving. In the stalls the seating was confined to benches, but up in the balcony there were actually individual seats. The front row was naturally reserved for the dignitaries.

The women in the audience were dressed splendidly. For most of them it was the one occasion in the year when they could show off their jewellery. The lights from the chandeliers caught the pearls and diamonds on display and their glitter added to the fairytale atmosphere of the evening.

The men had been forced to leave their guns in the lobby. The sheriff, having received the cable from Burke in Pinkerton's, had hastily sworn in a dozen deputies. These were now taking the revolvers away from the men as they arrived.

To while away the time a small orchestra was playing in the orchestra pit. They were actually playing some tunes from Alphonse's favourite operas. He had decided that, since he couldn't have an opera to open his opera house, at least he would include as much opera music as he could.

Some of Tooley's gang had already gone into the theatre. They were unrecognizable as the scruffy outlaws of a few days before. They had shaved and smartened them-selves up. They had gone up into the balcony where they had selected vantage points at the ends of the rows. Like the other men who had entered the theatre they had been forced to leave their guns behind in the safe-keeping of the deputies. However, unknown to the lawmen, they had small pistols concealed about their persons. These pistols, while not having the number of bullets of their Colts and not being able to fire as far, nevertheless could be lethal at short range.

There were four notable absentees from the outlaws in the balcony – Ben, Hillier, Tooley and Sylvia. They were waiting by the tethered horses in an alleyway close to the back of the theatre. The three men were waiting with eager anticipation. The fourth person, Sylvia, although outwardly calm, was inwardly trembling.

What was she doing here? Tooley hadn't explained why he had brought her along. She realized that it was all part of his plan to rob the audience inside. But what part had she to play in tonight's drama? Then there was Ben. He had gone willingly along with

Tooley's plan. She had thought that he had been a man who was basically good but had been the victim of cruel fate. But during these past few days she had revised her opinion. It had all started when he had calmly announced that he had been the father of this theatre-owner's wife's child. How could he? The woman was already married. He was an adulterer. Once he had confessed that fact she knew she could never regard him in the same light again. Whatever slight feelings of love she had felt for him had been dashed for ever.

During these past three days she had hardly spoken to him. Indeed it had been obvious to Tooley that something was amiss.

'What's the matter with you two?' he had asked on one occasion. 'Lover's quarrel?'

The coldness between himself and Sylvia suited Ben. He had deliberately dropped the bombshell about his relationship with Marie knowing that Sylvia would act the way she had done. She was an attractive young lady – a very attractive young lady, in fact. In other circumstances he wouldn't have hesitated to become better acquainted with her. It had hurt him to see the way she had deliberately distanced herself from him during these past days. She had even kept a certain distance away from him when they had been asleep on their solitary blanket.

But he had no doubt that his course of action was the right one. Tonight he was going to kill Hillier. He was going to avenge his father's death. It had to be tonight, since after the robbery the gang would all be hunted down. Not only the sheriff's men but Pinkerton's would be on their trail. He had caught sight of Grey in the front of the theatre. He guessed that one of Tooley's gang was a traitor. It was a pity he hadn't known that fact earlier, since he might have been able to approach him in secret. He might have been able to persuade the outlaw to get him a weapon. It was the one thing that was lacking in his plan. Tooley hadn't trusted him with one of those small guns which he had distributed to the rest of the gang.

'Do you think the show has started?' asked Tooley.

Ben listened intently. The music had stopped playing. It meant that the show had begun. He informed Tooley as much.

'We'll wait for ten minutes,' said Tooley, authoritatively, 'Then we'll move.'

The next ten minutes were the longest in Sylvia's life. She tried praying but while the church seemed to have prayers for all sorts of functions from christenings to weddings, they didn't seem to have prayers for waiting to go to rob a theatre. She glanced at Ben. His face was set and he was staring strangely at Hillier. Why was he staring at him, and with such an expression of dislike – no, hatred. Ben suddenly realized that she had been watching him and quickly turned his attention to the theatre door which was at the end of the alley.

What was the connection between Ben and Hillier? She racked her brains to try to come up with an answer. It must be something to do with Ben's past. She remembered how in court he had said that his father had been murdered. In fact it was that consideration which the judge had said had mitigated in his favour, and so he had reduced the sentence from the original figure to two years. Who had murdered Ben's father. Could it have been Hillier?

Once again she caught Ben glancing at the outlaw with the same look of undiluted hatred. She must be right. Hillier had murdered Ben's father. And now Ben was going to murder him. My God! It all fitted.

She wasn't aware that she had gasped aloud until the others turned.

'Don't be impatient,' said Tooley, with a sneer. 'It won't be long now.'

That was why Ben had gone along so readily with Tooley's plan. Probably that was why he had told her about his affair with the woman named Marie. There was no need for him to have told her. She would never have found out. He could easily have kept it a secret. But Ben had told her so that her feelings for him would become less. Ben had calculated that when he killed Hillier then the chances were his own life would come to an end as well.

This time her gasp was almost drowned by Tooley's order.

'Right, let's go,' he said.

The four approached the stage door. Tooley knocked on it. It was opened by a wizened old man. Tooley didn't hesitate. He brought the butt of his revolver crashing down on the old man's head. He sank to the floor without a groan.

Tooley stepped casually over the prone body, the others followed more circumspectly. They were in a corridor with several closed doors on either side. The corridor was deserted. Alphonse had built the theatre intending it to house opera stars and some of the dressing-rooms had a star painted on them.

There were several people in the wings. They were watching the first act – Charles

Lawson was on his second Shakespeare speech.

Be not afeard, the isle is full of noises.
Sounds and sweet airs that give delight
  and hurt not.
Sometimes a thousand twangling instru-
  ments
Will hum about mine ears...

The audience listened, spellbound. Tooley chose that moment to brush past the onlookers in the wings. He led his three companions on to the centre of the stage.

'I protest,' said Lawson. Tooley's answer was to shoot him. Lawson, dying, gave one of his best performances. He gasped several times, before finally collapsing on the stage.

Pandemonium broke out in the audi-torium. The deputies had drawn their guns. Before they could shoot, Tooley played his trump card. He held his gun at Sylvia's head.

'If anyone shoots, this young lady will die

as well.'

'It's my daughter,' cried a voice from the back of the audience. Many turned to see who was responsible for the outburst. They recognized the dog-collar of a minister.

'Nobody else will get hurt if you will give up your money and jewels to my men. This young lady will be returned safely to her father, I promise you,' shouted Tooley.

Realization dawned. The outlaws up in the balcony began collecting the men's pocket-books. There was some slight dissent, but if any man refused to part with his money his wife invariably entreated him to think of the poor girl on the stage and obey the outlaw. Everything seemed to be going according to plan. Tooley couldn't resist a smile of satisfaction.

'I'll go down among the audience in the stalls,' said Ben. 'I expect there'll be some pickings there.'

'Good idea,' said Tooley, casually.

Ben moved towards the wings. There were several steps leading down to the auditorium.

Before he reached them he had to pass a small table. It was a familiar table. He had stood by it on dozens of occasions. His throwing-knives had always been on that table. As they were now.

He stopped by the table. Tooley and Hillier were watching the outlaws collecting the valuables from the audience.

'Hillier,' Ben shouted out the name.

The outlaw swung round to face him.

'I'm going to give you the same chance you gave my father.' So saying Ben picked up one of the knives. In the same movement he threw it.

The knife hit Hillier in the centre of his heart. As another body joined Lawson on the stage Tooley turned to face Ben. Raw anger was stamped on his face at seeing the killing of his henchman. He swung his gun towards Ben. There was no way that Ben could grab a second knife in time. He knew his last moment had come. However Tooley wasn't able to get his clear shot since Sylvia, freed from the outlaw's grasp, responded by biting him on the hand. Tooley swung round to aim a blow at her. It gave Ben a split second of an advantage. He grabbed another knife. He flung it at Tooley at the same time as the outlaw swung back and fired at him.

Ben recovered slowly. It took him some time to realize he was lying in a bed. It didn't take him long, though, to realize that the pretty nurse sitting by his bed was Sylvia.

'You're awake,' she cried.

'What happened?' a voice croaked. Was it his?

'Would you like a drink?'

'Yes, please.'

She held a glass of water for him. It tasted like nectar.

'What happened?' he repeated. This time in a stronger voice.

'You killed the two outlaws, Hillier and Tooley.'

'I remember killing Hillier. I think you had a lot to do with me killing Tooley.'

'I only put him off his aim. His bullets managed to find your shoulder. You lost a lot of blood. Luckily it missed your heart.'

'You still helped to save my life. I can't thank you enough.'

'That's nonsense,' she said, sharply. 'You're still delirious.'

He stared at her. She met his gaze un-flinchingly.

'You're beautiful,' he said. This time the huskiness in his voice was caused by emotion.

She blushed. 'You'll be pleased to know that you won't have to go back to jail,' she stated. 'Your sentence has been rescinded in view of the way you helped to bring Tooley's gang to justice.'

'So I'll be free to go when I can get up?'

'I suppose so.' She regarded him steadily.

'When will that be?'

'It'll be up to the doctor. In a week or so perhaps.'

'When that time comes I have one favour to ask of you.'

'What's that?'

'Will you walk out with me?'

She didn't reply straightaway. She wasn't going to refuse, was she? Her answer was to lean over and kiss him.

'I'll take that as a yes,' he said.

The publishers hope that this book has given you enjoyable reading. Large Print Books are especially designed to be as easy to see and hold as possible. If you wish a complete list of our books please ask at your local library or write directly to:

Dales Large Print Books
Magna House, Long Preston,
Skipton, North Yorkshire.
BD23 4ND

This Large Print Book, for people
who cannot read normal print,
is published under the auspices of
THE ULVERSCROFT FOUNDATION

... we hope you have enjoyed this book.
Please think for a moment about those
who have worse eyesight than you ...
and are unable to even read or enjoy
Large Print without great difficulty.

You can help them by sending a
donation, large or small, to:

**The Ulverscroft Foundation,
1, The Green, Bradgate Road,
Anstey, Leicestershire, LE7 7FU,
England.**
or request a copy of our brochure for
more details.

The Foundation will use all donations
to assist those people who are visually
impaired and need special attention
with medical research, diagnosis
and treatment.

Thank you very much for your help.